DALLAS' RIDE

C. G. SALO

JULY 10/20

Debbie
This proves you're
never too old!
Carolyn

 FriesenPress

Suite 300 - 990 Fort St
Victoria, BC, V8V 3K2
Canada

www.friesenpress.com

ISBN
978-1-5255-6253-2(Hardcover)
978-1-5255-6254-9 (Paperback)
978-1-5255-6255-6(eBook)

1. FICTION, ROMANCE, ACTION & ADVENTURE

Distributed to the trade by The Ingram Book Company

DALLAS' RIDE

CHAPTER 1

DID YOU EVER wake up and just know that the day was going to be a disaster?

It was already 11:30 a.m., and Dallas knew she would never make it to *Rev It Up* by the noon deadline to drop off her entry form for the NSDE motorcycle race. She'd always loved motorcycle racing, and when she found out about this race, she was interested – very interested. She wanted to test her skills and prove to herself that she was as good a rider as she thought.

She could have been on her way a lot sooner, but Grandma Nolan had picked this morning of all mornings to discuss Rosemary Weidermeyer's gall bladder surgery in all its gory details. *Then,* she dropped the bomb that *she* was planning on entering this race herself. Their breakfast conversation replayed in her head...

"I know you're worried about my ability to run this race, but trust me, Grams, I know what I'm doing."

"Well then. I guess that's that."

Her grandmother paused for effect and then reached across the table and took Dallas' hand.

"The only thing I can say now is...when do *we* sign up?"

"Wait a minute, Grams..."

"No. Don't 'Grams' me. I can ride with the best of them or at least I could twenty years ago. If there are two of us entered in this dang-faggled race, the chances of us winning are even better."

"That's true, but..."

"There are no buts about it. I'm entering this race, and that's all there is to it. This old gal needs some excitement in her life. God knows, living with your grandfather I didn't get too much of that.

Looking towards the heavens she muttered, "God rest his soul." Grandma Nolan never let her short stature or her age stop her from tackling any challenge – especially when someone said she couldn't do it.

Dallas stifled a sigh. Talking her grandmother out of this would be like trying to talk an elephant down from a lamppost.

The National Six-Day Endurance race was one of the jewels in the motorcycle racers' circuit and was by far the toughest, most demanding motorcycle race of its kind. Dallas knew her grandmother didn't have what it would take to start, let alone finish. She wasn't even sure that with all her *own* racing experience, *she* had what it took.

It was best just to humor Grams; Dallas would come up with a way to dissuade her later.

In the midst of all that, the office called to say that Billy Ray wouldn't have her SUV fixed until late that afternoon. Dallas told her secretary, Betty, that wasn't acceptable. She needed the vehicle to do her patrols. Betty just laughed and reminded Dallas that nothing short of a major earthquake could make

Billy Ray do anything faster than he planned, *and* they hadn't had an earthquake in Desire, Colorado since…well, never.

That left her with three options for transportation: her Yamaha V-Star, her Yamaha TW200, which she would prefer not to use until she had made some adjustments to it for the race, or Grandma Nolan's 1949 Desoto.

Dallas' luck continued to suck because *it* had a flat tire. So, the Yamaha V-Star it was.

Twenty minutes later, she screeched into the parking lot of Rev It Up. Dallas parked in front of the shop, the official *headquarters* for this year's National Six-Day Endurance Race. She still couldn't believe that the NSDE officials had chosen Dallas' charming little town of Desire as the start point for the race.

Desire, Colorado wasn't renowned as a town on anyone's must-visit list. It was a pleasant enough place to pass through with its quaint clapboard and gingerbread houses and a main street right out of a small-town USA handbook. It even had a town square complete with a band shell. People here were laid back and friendly, and most everyone knew each other. If you had a mind to stop for a spell, it would most likely be at Emma's Grill for a quick home-cooked meal on your way to anywhere else. Some people just stopped to take in the breathtaking panorama of the Colorado Rockies rising up from the foothills surrounding the town.

Dallas wasn't paying any attention to the view as she raced up the steps into the reception area of Rev It Up. The dark paneled walls held pictures of every make and model of motorcycle known to man. Motorcycle memorabilia and custom motorcycle parts and accessories covered every square inch of the showroom. Dallas fingered a leather jacket with a Yamaha insignia on the back but quickly decided it was too rich for her blood when she got a glimpse of the price tag.

She waved to J.T. MacKay, the NSDE race coordinator, who was sitting at one of the two desks that occupied the room. Dallas removed her black helmet as she approached him.

"How's it going J.T.?"

J.T. looked up just as Dallas shook loose her beautiful auburn hair. He watched mesmerized as the red waves floated around her face and down her back. He always felt like a tongue-tied schoolboy whenever she was around. Her striking beauty caused his heart to do back flips.

Dallas was a well-put-together package at five foot eight, divided equally between gorgeous long legs and a well-endowed and well-toned upper body, but it was her face that stopped traffic. Her eyes were the color of Irish shamrocks. A smattering of freckles dusted the bridge of her slightly up-turned nose, enhancing her creamy skin. Funny enough, she always seemed oblivious to the effect she had on the opposite sex.

J.T. had a hard time focusing on what he was doing. He'd always harbored strong feelings for Dallas; feelings he knew didn't run as deep with her. They were good friends, and he accepted that.

J.T. took a moment longer admiring her as she stood at his desk with her helmet under her arm. Her red hair curled damply around her face, her eyes sparkling with the energy of her smile.

She could easily be the centerfold for *Playboy* – even fully dressed in black leathers.

"Hey Dallas, out chasing bad guys?" he said picking his tongue up off the floor.

"About time you got here; another twenty-five minutes and you would have been out of luck. I'm glad you changed your mind about entering."

For a time, Dallas had considered it unprofessional of her to enter the race, but J.T. convinced her otherwise. He said it would look good on her and show that she truly was a part of the community. He knew that Dallas would have the citizens of Desire hooked if she participated.

Unzipping her leather jacket, she reached inside and pulled out her registration form.

"I've decided to enter. I gave it some serious thought, and I know I can do this. Oh, by the way Grandma Nolan's entering too."

"Yah right."

"No, I'm serious. She decided she needed to spice up her life, but when she comes in, tell her there's an age limit or something."

"I can't do that Dallas. There is no age limit. If you've got a bike and license, you can ride." He took Dallas' form and laid it on the pile on his desk.

"I didn't know your grandmother knew how to ride a motorcycle. Does she even have a bike?"

"She does if you call a 1949 Indian with no tires a bike."

Dallas checked her watch. Only twenty more minutes to the deadline. Maybe Grandma Nolan wouldn't make it in time.

Thank God!

She knew Grams didn't have any transportation because she

had left the Desoto with the flat. That made Dallas feel better. It meant there was no way Grams could get here on time.

Just as she was heaving a sigh of relief, the bell over the door to the bike shop jingled merrily. Dallas didn't have to turn around. She just knew it was Grams coming through the door.

"Am I too late to enter?" Grandma Nolan wheezed, trying to catch her breath.

"I didn't think I would make it in time. There's something wrong with the Desoto; it ran awful funny on the way over here. Couldn't seem to keep it going straight. Must need a tune-up or something."

Dallas turned her face toward the heavens. *Lord, help me.*

"Grams, the Desoto had a flat tire. You didn't really drive it all the way over here, did you?"

"Well, damn. No wonder it ran funny."

Dallas could just imagine what the tire and rim looked like now. *Guess I'll have to get Billy Ray to come and tow it to his garage.* She listened as Grams babbled on about the race and how excited she was to be entering.

Grandma Nolan's voice always took on a high pitched, screechy tone when she was excited, and judging by the timber at this moment, Dallas knew she was in seventh heaven.

J.T. couldn't help it. Between the look on Dallas' face and the fire-engine-red, tattered leather jacket Grandma Nolan had on over her buttercup-yellow stretch pants he lost it.

It was a good minute before the scowling faces of Dallas and her grandmother brought him out of his fit of laughter.

"No, Grandma Nolan." J.T. just couldn't keep the laughter out of his voice. "You're right on time."

J.T. accepted her application, his body trembling from the effort it took not to burst out laughing again.

Dallas glared at him.

"*J.T.,* don't you have something to tell Grandma Nolan?" she said winking her eye conspiratorially.

"Uh, no. It looks like everything is in order. She's even ended her signature with a little skull and crossbones. Nice touch, Grandma Nolan."

J.T. was an impressive package with his sun-streaked hair and honey-colored eyes. Even the limp he was left with after a suspect's bullet ended his career as an FBI agent didn't detract from his appealing good looks, but at this moment, Dallas had the urge to paste him one for letting her grandmother enter the race.

She heaved a sigh of acceptance. If circumstances had been different, she could really be attracted to J.T, but after all the grief and unanticipated changes that had happened in her life lately, she couldn't see herself throwing a relationship into the mix.

Her grandfather's recent death and her new job still had her reeling. Still, his boyish good looks and surfer/body-builder physique would turn any woman's head. Put that together with his great personality and business sense, and you had a package made in heaven. Any women would have tripped over herself trying to get close to him – any woman that is but Dallas.

Right at that moment, she would like nothing better than to disconnect his head from his shoulders.

"You know J.T., it can be very dangerous out on the mean streets of Desire. I'd be looking over my shoulder from now on if I were you," she said in the way of a threat.

J.T. knew Dallas was miffed, but there really was nothing

he could do. Grandma Nolan's application was in order, and if she really could ride and had a motorcycle, he couldn't stop her from entering.

He also knew that Dallas was kidding. Wasn't she?

In her newly appointed position with the town of Desire, she *could* cause him some trouble, but he knew she was above reproach and would never do anything unlawful. Playing along with her threat he countered.

"I'll keep that in mind."

Besides his duties as NSDE race coordinator, J.T. was also one of the owners of Rev It Up, a chain of businesses that customized motorcycles, and the president of the local Motorcycle Association.

J.T. believed that some people were born to ride, and Dallas was one of them. She sat on a bike like she was relaxing in a comfortable rocking chair, and it was because of her ability on a motorcycle that J.T. had suggested that Dallas enter the NSDE race.

Dallas had read the pamphlets and articles J.T. had given her about the race and decided she was up for the challenge.

It was the most demanding endurance race in the United States. Each day consisted of up to 150 miles of on-road and off-road runs. A few of the days even had timed, ten-mile motocross courses tacked on to the end, just for added stress. The routes were through sand, mud, water, and mountains – whatever the terrain dictated. Each rider was timed to the second. One minute past the latest predetermined time for each leg, and you were out of the race. Period.

Repairs to the motorcycles were made on the fly, and the rider was the only one who could perform them. Heat, rain, sleet, and cold all took their toll on riders and the bikes; all this for the thrill of the win.

Dallas knew that the six days would mean that her deputies would have to take on the lion's share of her work, and it would take every ounce of her talent and strength, but she was a carbon copy of her grandmother. She would attempt any test put in her path.

The first prize in the NSDE was ten thousand dollars, and even though the money would be a nice perk, it was not the only reason she was attempting this race. She wanted to prove to herself that she could do this.

Once she had made up her mind to enter, her one and only question to J.T. had been if a woman had ever won, or even come close. J.T. had to admit that no, a female never had…yet. But on two separate occasions they had placed second.

Dallas had still hemmed and hawed over entering but only for about five seconds. She *couldn't* win if she didn't enter, and Dallas was always up for a challenge.

After discussing some details about what equipment she would need to take to the race and how the race was run, Dallas escaped the shop, leaving J.T. and her grandmother arguing over his insinuation that she might be a little too old to ride in such a strenuous race.

That got Grandma Nolan madder than a wet hen.

"Now you listen here, Jeremy Theodore MacKay." Grandma Nolan was one of the few people J.T. would let get away with calling him by his given name.

"I'm not too old for anything. Besides I've been riding motorcycles since you were a pup."

"My point exactly, Grandma Nolan. Don't you think…"

"Don't try and smart talk me sonny. I'll show all you young-sters how a pro rides a bike. Now just sign me up.

Dallas didn't feel the least bit sorry leaving J.T. with Grandma Nolan. He knew better than to get into a discussion about anything with her grandmother. She was always right, and everyone else was always wrong.

Dallas did up her jacket, pulled on her gloves and helmet, and started her Yamaha. She loved the purr of the engine. Closing her eyes, she let the sound and the vibration course through her body. Straddling the bike like she would a lover, Dallas put up the kickstand and revved the engine. She popped the clutch, shifted into gear, and the bike surged forward. The front wheel lifted off the ground a few inches then bit into the pavement, launching her forward down the driveway and into the intersection – never slowing her speed.

Dallas caught a brief glimpse of the black Harley-Davidson as she pulled out of the driveway into oncoming traffic. Realizing she had probably come a little close, she pulled over on the shoulder to make sure the rider was okay. That's when her day went from bad to worse.

Braking to avoid a collision, the vintage Harley and its rider went down in a shower of sparks. Connor O'Reilly found himself sliding sideways along the pavement, the sound of scraping metal grating in his ears. Over the roar of the scream-ing engine came the expletive: "Son of a bitch!"

Connor stayed with the bike longer than he should have, hoping to minimize the damage to the $5000 paint job he'd just done to the bike. But that judgment call left no room for escape.

Cursing a blue streak, Connor lay there with the weight of the bike resting heavily against his leg. The heat from the exhaust pipe started to seep through his leathers. Every movement Connor made gave him pain. He tried shaking his throbbing head to clear his vision, but that only increased his discomfort.

Slowly, his head cleared and through the swirling dust kicked up by the warm, late summer breeze, Connor spotted a lone black-clad figure. Raising himself up on one elbow, he tried to bring the doubled image together, but the figure kept wavering in the haze of heat rising from the pavement. It took all of Connor's concentration and strength to finally get to his feet. Pain shot up his leg when he attempted to put his weight on it. He sucked in his breath, but this only succeeded in opening up the split on his lip a little farther. Blood trickled into his mouth, and the coppery taste fueled his fury.

He knew this phantom apparition was the cause of his agony and anger and when he reached the guy, he was going to make him pay. He was furious, but he knew losing control was not where he wanted to go right now. Taking deep calming breaths, he got himself reasonably composed.

He wouldn't think about all the money that he had just spent customizing the Harley.

He wouldn't think about the cost of repairs that would come out of his pocket – again.

He wouldn't think about the injury to his leg, but he would think about what he was going to do to the idiot who had just cut him off.

"When I get my hands on that son-of-a-bitch I'll throttle him to within an inch of his life," he muttered.

Righting the motorcycle, he ran his hand over the long, ugly scrape that marred the midnight-black finish of the Harley. His brow furled. The frown changed his features from tough to terrifying. He turned towards the soon-to-be pulverized prick, ready to hammer him into the ground.

Dallas Nolan firmly believed that first impressions were lasting ones. That being the case, this one was going to last a very long time.

Limping towards her was the biggest, meanest, sexiest-looking man she had ever seen. The fact that he looked mad as hell did little to change her first impression, and the fact that she was the reason he looked that way made her just a little nervous.

At five foot eight, Dallas had always considered herself above average in height, but standing toe to toe with this mountain of a man was giving her a neck cramp.

He had to be six foot four if he was an inch, and right now, every inch of him was poised over her like a cobra ready to strike. The few stands of wavy black hair that the gentle summer breeze blew across his tanned cheeks did little to soften the hard planes of his face.

Dallas was tempted, but only for a split second, to tuck them behind his ear. As if guessing her thoughts, his full sensuous lips curled into a snarl, and Dallas could have sworn that she heard him growl.

He growled. Like some half-rabid animal! If he was trying to intimidate her – well, he almost succeeded.

Dallas stood her ground – not because she was all that brave, but because eyes the color of Arctic ice had frozen her to the spot.

How could someone who looked that devastatingly gorgeous in black leather make her feel like what he wanted most in life was her head on a platter?

"You idiot! Where the hell did you learn how to ride?" he bellowed.

Dallas' back went up. Who did this guy think he was yelling at? Some local yokel?

"Hey, settle down buddy. Just drop by the Sheriff's office, and we'll settle this over there."

Her voice was muffled by the full-face visor on her helmet. Dallas hadn't been inclined to lift the faceplate and actually make direct eye contact. This wasn't her first encounter with a potentially dangerous individual, but she didn't want to push her luck by being a hero. What she wanted was to make sure that he was on her turf, where she had plenty of backup if things went south.

"You're damn right we will, boy! I know the way. I'll meet you there."

Boy? Does he think I'm a guy? Hmm. This could prove interesting. That thought made her smile. She had a few tricks she could show him.

Dallas was used to meeting aggression up close, even though the hardest thing she had to do since returning to Desire as the newly appointed Sheriff was to roust some drunks from the local bar. Still, this guy looked like he wanted to chew her up and spit her out. Dallas knew she could handle herself if she had to, but why press her luck when she could have Jimmy Bob Horner and Ralph Tewlittle backing her up?

Connor limped back to his bike and put up the kickstand.

This juvenile delinquent is going to learn that you don't mess with Connor O'Reilly or his bike, he thought – but first he had to register for the NSDE.

CHAPTER 2

J.T. AND SOME of the employees of Rev It Up had watched from the window in absolute horror as Connor dumped his bike.

"Oh shit," someone whispered.

Everyone held their breath as Connor slowly got up and checked to make sure he had all his parts and they were all in working order. Gently lifting the bike, he did a thorough inspection, but the look on his face told all inside the shop that the bike had not fared as well as the rider.

A ripple of sympathy went out to poor Dallas. In unison, everyone took a step back from the window. Their fear of Connor's reaction was palpable.

Connor and J.T. had become fast friends over the years, enjoying the shared camaraderie of motorcycles and law enforcement. Connor O'Reilly was an FBI agent stationed in Pueblo. His love of motorcycles had brought him to J.T.'s bike shop almost five years ago. Jake Myers, another FBI agent and riding enthusiast, had turned him on to J.T.'s shop saying it was the best in the Western United States.

He had been right.

Connor began bringing all of his bikes to J.T. for

customizing, and when he found out that J.T. was struggling financially, Connor became a silent partner.

They had first met during the murder investigation that had ended J.T.'s career. A cornered gunman had let loose with a barrage from a M16 assault rifle when J.T. had tried to approach him. One bullet went through J.T.'s chest; the other shattered his femur. It was only by the grace of God and some very talented surgeons that J.T. had survived. After a very long recovery, the powers that be insisted that J.T. had given enough to his country and put him on semi-retired status, but they still called on him whenever they needed his profiling expertise.

After his recovery was complete, J.T. found he had too much time on his hands, so he decided to pursue his love of motorcycles by opening Rev It Up.

Because of his looks, Connor turned heads everywhere he went. He had what could only be described as Hollywood-leading-man good looks. The old cliché "tall, dark, and handsome" fit him to a T. Once you met Connor O'Reilly, you never forgot him.

How he could work as an undercover FBI Agent was mind-boggling, yet he was known as one of the best. Connor wasn't the type of person who could fade into the background, but his persona demanded that he be treated with caution and respect, and it was that fact that had the women in J.T.'s office letting out a collective sigh.

"Oh, give me a break," J.T. muttered. "You won't be standing there sighing like a bunch of love-sick school girls when he comes storming through that door."

Connor was every woman's dream. His brooding handsome looks affected every woman the same way. Jet-black hair, left long to brush over his collar, curled slightly at the ends. Any red-blooded woman would give her life savings to be able to run their fingers through it. His blue eyes could be as calm as a lake in the summer or as stormy as a tempest on the ocean. Some of his female conquests said, "If you stared into them for too long, you were likely to drown in their depths."

Full sensual lips hid a beautiful set of perfect teeth, and his smile, which was a rare occurrence, could devastate a woman.

Connor's height coupled with a well-muscled physique had each of the ladies imagining herself wrapped in his powerful embrace. Connor could make a woman melt in his arms or the meanest thug think twice before confronting him. He used both to his advantage when the occasion called for it.

Connor's temper was also well known to each and everyone of the staff, and because of that, none of them wanted to be there when he came through the door. Suddenly thinking of pressing matters each of them had to attend to, they scurried off in all directions leaving J.T. to face Connor alone.

"Uh, I think I hear the phone," one of the most cowardly of the group muttered.

"Yep, there goes line two. Don't worry I'll get it," someone else said.

"Cowards," J.T. taunted.

Expletives rang through the air as Connor limped up the walkway pushing the Harley. Fixing the kickstand, he stomped up the stairs and slammed the door back with his clenched fist, almost driving it through the glass storefront.

Fury still radiated from him as he stormed up to the registration desk and hammered his hands down on the well-worn solid oak counter. He looked J.T. straight in the eye and bellowed, "Who the hell was that idiot?"

Rage drove him as he hobbled back and forth in front of the desks, ranting. "I just spent three damn months restoring that bike. Do you know how many hours that is? I'll tell you how many...too many!

"That's five thousand dollars down the tubes and for what? For some stupid, careless bastard, who doesn't know his ass from a crankshaft, let alone how to ride a bike, to totally destroy it in five seconds."

J.T. suppressed a devilish grin. He'd never seen Connor dump a bike before, and it dawned on him that Connor wouldn't appreciate knowing who the rider was that had caused him to do it.

"If you'd calm down..."

"Calm down! You expect me to calm down?"

"If I could get a word in edgewise, I'll tell you who that idiot was..."

"I don't need a name!" he roared. "I just need to know where he lives so I can kick his sorry ass."

Whoa, wait a minute, J.T. thought. *Connor thinks that was a guy.* He decided to play along,

"Name's Dallas Nolan, just finished registering for the race."

Stopping in mid-stride, Connor stood there staring at J.T. in disbelief. He wasn't hearing right.

He was going to be racing against that idiot.

Chewing on that thought, he reached inside his leather jacket and shoved the form across the counter.

"Here! I can't believe you actually allowed that moron to enter the race."

"Yup, you register, you race."

Snickering to himself, J.T. knew he was going to really enjoy the showdown that was coming. Unable to restrain himself, J.T. was now actually laughing out loud.

"What the hell is so funny?"

J.T. knew exactly how Connor was going to react when he found out that Dallas Nolan was a woman, but he wasn't going to be the one to tell him. He also knew Connor wouldn't appreciate another bout of laughter, so he just shrugged his shoulders.

Mr. O'Reilly had a great deal of respect for women as long as they were in short skirts, tight tops, and on the back of a bike – not the rider of one.

J.T. had seen women literally fall at Connor's feet only to have him step over them. He treated them with indifference that some might say he had reason to. He had tried the marriage scene once, but it didn't take. His ex-wife, Catherine, almost bankrupt him with her divorce settlement. Up to that point, Connor's respect for women had been shaky at best. His mother ran out on him and his father when Connor was only five years old. She had said she needed to live the *"great adventure"*, whatever the hell that meant. She had abandoned her husband and son, never to be seen again.

No letters, no phone calls, just gone.

Living with his father's constant negative attitude towards women had rubbed off on Connor, but he had thought Catherine was different. The problem was that she turned out to be worse than his mother. Connor's mother had left taking nothing. Catherine had left with everything, including his heart.

After the divorce, his respect for women was all but non-existent.

Following Connor's divorce and J.T.'s retirement from the FBI, they turned to their common interest in motorcycles and racing, but not together. J.T. opened Rev It Up, and Connor buried himself in his work. A few years later, Connor had showed up on his doorstep wanting a bike customized. The rest was history.

"Are we finished here? I've gotta get to the Sheriff's office so that I can wring that idiot's neck."

"Yup. We're done," J.T. said, filing Connor's entrance form with the others. "I was going to discuss the last quarter returns with you, but that can wait. It's good and that should be enough info for now."

"Good luck with your neck-wringing," J.T. said, trying to keep the grin off his face.

"I hope I won't have to bail you out later," he added under his breath.

CHAPTER 3

CONNOR WAS STILL pissed that the idiot who had cut him off was entered in the race. If this Dallas Nolan couldn't even follow a few simple traffic rules, how in hell was he going to run in the NSDE race? This race took concentration and skill, and it was quite obvious that Nolan lacked both those qualities.

Connor heaved a sigh. He had the distinct impression that Dallas Nolan spelled trouble.

Spotting the Sheriff's office less than a quarter of a mile away, Connor pulled his thoughts back to how pissed off he was and how much he wanted to tear a strip off of Nolan's hide.

Parking the badly scraped Harley and still favoring his leg, Connor limped toward the front doors of the station – if you could call it that. The Sheriff's office was actually an old Victorian home that had been converted into offices for the local law enforcement.

In truth, it looked more like the gingerbread house in the old "Hansel and Gretel" fairytale, which was laughable at best. Connor couldn't help himself. What did they do with law-breakers? Bake them chocolate-chip cookies until they confessed? Unbelievable!

Over the door were two intricately carved, hand-painted

signs. The first one identified the house as the local Sheriff's Office and stated that Buck Williams was the town Sheriff. The second one told Connor to "Please wipe his feet before entering."

Give me a break, Connor thought to himself. He looked around to see if anyone was watching and purposely stepped over the "Welcome" mat.

As he pulled open the door, he heard chimes ring through the station. *Chimes! What the hell were these people thinking?*

He walked towards the reception desk and there sat Betty – at least that's what her nametag said.

"Hey there, Betty."

Best to treat these people like he was one of them.

"Is Dallas around?"

Betty looked up at the stranger slack-jawed. She was only slightly taken aback at the familiarity in his tone towards her but was positively stunned by his utter…beauty.

The man was gorgeous.

"Dallas?" She said in the form of a question.

"Yah, you know, Dallas Nolan. I'm supposed to meet him here."

Betty let the reference of Dallas being referred to as a 'he' slide by for the moment.

"Well now," Betty replied regaining her composure.

"Dallas got called out to Mrs. Ruttabaker's house. Seems like she found her husband dead. Claimed he was hanging from the ceiling fan in her living room."

Connor didn't even attempt a reply to her declaration. He stood there totally stunned by her statement. He couldn't believe how blasé Betty sounded about the suggested suicide.

Who was Mrs. Ruttabaker and why was Betty acting so unconcerned about the poor woman's husband?

Better still, why was Dallas Nolan called out to the scene of an attempted suicide? He was beginning to feel like he was in the *Twilight Zone* or something.

Betty noticed the shock on Mr. Gorgeous' face and suppressed a chuckle.

"Well now, don't go getting all in a kerfuffle, young man. Mr. Ruttabaker isn't really hanging from the living-room ceiling fan. You see, Mrs. Ruttabaker is a few sandwiches shy of a picnic. She likes to call in every so often to let us know that the mister's passed away, even though it's been over seven years since he crossed over. Her mind isn't quite what it used to be, you see. After her dear old husband died, her mind flew South for the winter and decided never to come back. Such a shame.

"So we go out to her place every couple of weeks or so, play out the scene, have one of her homemade cookies, give her a shot of good old Dr. Jack Daniels, and leave."

Connor was still speechless. Where did these people learn to talk –the Redneck School for Bumbling Idiots?

"Uh, I was supposed to meet Nolan here, will this take long?" He didn't want to spend his afternoon waiting when he had work of his own to do.

"Shouldn't take too long. It's just a matter of calming Mrs. Ruttabaker down. That usually only takes one or two glasses of whiskey. She likes to tipple you see."

"No kidding," Connor said under his breath.

"I'll just sit here and wait then."

Connor gave Betty one of his rare smiles and then turned

around and sat down on the overstuffed, flowered sofa with the little crocheted doilies on the arms.

Are you kidding me? he thought as he sat.

It took Betty a full minute to recover from Connor's smile. No one had ever smiled at her like that before. She felt like she had just won the lottery or was some kind of princess or something. It made a person want to stand up and sing.

And that's exactly what she did.

Suddenly, Connor's ears were assailed by the most god-awful sound he had ever heard, and it was coming from Betty. She was singing at the top of her lungs – or more precisely, caterwauling – to a Shania Twain tune about "feeling like a woman."

Connor thought she sounded like a tomcat out cruising.

He tried blocking out the cacophony, but when that didn't work, he looked around for something to occupy his time. The only thing available was a copy of *Home and Country.*

He blindly thumbed through the pages while he envisioned how he was going to dissect Dallas Nolan, not only for destroying his Harley, but for leaving him with this Okie from Muskogee.

He still didn't understand what the biker from hell was doing at a "suicide" scene, but there were only two possibilities that he could think of: One, Dallas was the local coroner. Or two, and God forbid, Nolan was the rookie cop of the decade. Either way, it didn't matter; things weren't looking too good for old Dallas.

Dallas wasn't even thinking about her little "accident" this morning. She was trying to console a distraught Mrs.

Ruttabaker. She poured Ethel another shot of Jack Daniels and handed it to the shaking woman.

One had to pretend that the event in question had actually just taken place.

"You don't have to worry about his legs getting in the way of the television, Mrs. Ruttabaker. We've taken your husband down from the ceiling fan. I know it must have frightened you to find him there this morning."

If you tried to convince Mrs. Ruttabaker that her husband wasn't actually hanging from the living room ceiling, she would become even more distressed. As macabre as it sounded, it was better to let her believe that he was deceased in the living room right now instead of dead and buried for over seven years.

"Thank you, dear. He gave me an awful fright just hanging there like that. There I was, watching *Jerry Springer*. You know, they were talking about women having affairs with their mothers' sister's boyfriends today, and these two women got down right uppity about it and started going at each other tooth and nail. Got me so wound up I needed a little touch of my medicine to calm my heart. I was only gone long enough for a little nip and to make myself a cup of tea. When I got back, well, there he was just hanging there." Her hand shook as she pointed to the ceiling fan.

Dallas suppressed a sigh. Something had to be done about Mrs. Ruttabaker. Her phone calls regarding her husband were getting more frequent, and she was tying up too much of their time. Dallas knew they had to follow procedure whenever someone called the station, but enough was enough. After the NSDE was finished, she'd have to have a serious talk with 'Doc' Wambaugh about her.

If they didn't attend at the scene and something happened to Mrs. R., Dallas and her whole team would incur the wrath of the town. Everyone knew Mrs. Ruttabaker was a brick short of a full load, but just in case it was a true emergency, they had to respond. Her family had up and left, and no one wanted to claim responsibility for the poor woman.

It was a real shame.

"Do you think I could have another glass, just for medicinal purposes, my dear? Just for my nerves? You understand."

Dallas shook herself out of her reverie in time to see Ethel handing her a now empty glass and asking for more.

What's the harm? she thought.

"Now that he's gone, you don't have to sit with me. I'll just watch *Dr. Phil* now. I'm sure I'll be fine. Just don't forget to pour that drink, please, and you can leave the bottle right here next to me, dear, just in case."

Dallas poured another shot and watched as Mrs. Ruttabaker tossed it back, wobbled a little unsteadily, and then passed out cold on the sofa.

It just broke her heart knowing that this woman had no one. The townspeople liked her well enough, but no one was willing to do more for her than bake the occasional pie.

People in small towns usually were overly friendly, but in the case of Mrs. Ruttabaker, they just seemed to want to mind their own business.

Dallas let herself out and walked to her cruiser. She thought back to her Grams, which then led her to think about the race. And that reminded her she was supposed to meet the "man in black" at the station. Just thinking of him shot a shiver of excitement mixed with dread through her.

"Shit!"

He had been furious with her at the scene of the little fender bender, but now he was going to be spitting fire because of her lengthy delay.

She took off for the office, leaving a cloud of dust in her wake.

On the one hand she hoped he would still be there, so she could get another look at him. But, on the other hand, she hoped he was gone. She really didn't want to deal with him right now.

CHAPTER 4

DALLAS CAME RUSHING through the front door of the Sheriff's office and skidded to a halt in front of Betty's desk.

"Land sakes, Sheriff! You damn near made me swallow my gum. Where's the fire?" Betty asked Dallas.

"And by the way, that was one fine hunk of meat you had sitting here for the better part of forty minutes."

"What did you do with him, Betty? Did you lock him in a cell? And I've told you a hundred times not to call me Sheriff!"

"Why the hell not? That's what you are. And no, I didn't lock him in a cell, although it surely did cross my mind. Lands sake, that boy set my pulse all aflutter.

"But I will say he was downright angry when he stormed off a few minutes ago. He said something about you not having the guts to settle your little dispute like a man. What do ya think he meant by that Dallas? Anyway, he said something about sending you a bill."

Dallas was just fine with that. She didn't relish meeting the man face to face again anyhow. He was so pissed off with her, she was sure he'd want a chunk of her ass before payment for the damage to his motorcycle.

Dallas had enough things on her mind right now with

having just been appointed Sheriff of this town by way of the backdoor.

Why did Buck have to die anyway? He was a young man – 73 at last count. So what if he liked to drink a little too much and he liked younger women? It shouldn't have affected his health like that.

Dallas had taken a position as deputy with the Desire Sheriff's department twelve months ago. She had just finished college with a degree in law enforcement. When the deputy position opened up, she jumped on it. But now, here she was, the reluctant head honcho.

She took a deep breath. She hadn't been prepared to take on the responsibilities of the town sheriff – but the town, like the people in it, was her responsibility now, and she took that responsibility seriously.

"Okay, Betty, what other crisis do we have to tackle today?"

"Well now, Billy Ray called to say that the station wagon was ready to be picked up…"

Dallas tuned Betty out. She was used to listening to the mundane goings-on in a small town; it was mostly just gossip anyhow.

She tuned her out, that is, until she heard the word "FBI".

"Whoa! Back up a minute. What's that about the FBI, Betty?" Dallas interrupted.

"Well now, if you were paying attention, and don't think for a minute I didn't know you weren't, you woulda heard me say that the FBI called and some agent left a message. Something about that motorcycle race that's going on here."

"What else did they say?" Dallas couldn't quite keep the interest from her voice.

"Well now, not much. Just a name and number for you to call."

Dallas grabbed at the slip of paper in Betty's hand and rushed to her office. Why couldn't Betty lead with the important stuff instead of wasting her time with the nonsense that goes on in Desire?

Dallas closed the door to her office, picked up the phone, and dialed the number. Her hands were shaking. She didn't know why she was so nervous. After all, she only calling the *Federal Bureau of Investigation!*

Right!

This was just another event in the long line of weirdness that had gone on today. With the way her luck was going today, they were probably calling to tell her that Grams was the head of the Hell's Angels or something equally as bizarre and that they'd finally caught up with her.

"Agent Fuller, please," Dallas replied when the receptionist asked who she would like to speak to.

"Special Agent Fuller here."

Dallas nearly jumped out of her chair and looked over her shoulder. It sounded like he was right there in the room with her because he had such a deep, powerful voice.

Get a grip, Dallas.

Great! Now she was getting paranoid and thinking that *they* were watching *her*.

"Uh, Agent Fuller. Dallas Nolan here from Desire. I'm returning your call."

"Oh yes, Sheriff Nolan."

Dallas cringed at hearing herself being called "Sheriff".

"Thanks for getting back to me so quickly."

"No problem. What can I do for you?" Dallas wondered what the hell she could possibly do for the FBI.

"The Bureau would like to enlist your help in an investigation. Have you read anything about the Heirloom Bandit?"

"Yes, as a matter of fact, I have, Agent Fuller. But what's that got to do with me?"

"Well now, we believe that the person responsible for these robberies has been using the motorcycle racing circuit as his format for casing out and pulling off his heists. And since the NSDE is being run from your town, we would like to enlist your help in this regard. We have tried contacting the local law in each of the towns where these races take place, hoping to be a step ahead of him, but so far we've had no luck with finding out who he is or apprehending him."

Dallas gathered her thoughts for a moment. She admitted to herself that she didn't like how the job of Sheriff had been foisted on her, but she'd be damned if she was going to let the FBI run a show in her town without her input or help. She had gotten the job by default, but she knew that she was damn good at it.

"Well, l if you don't mind, Special Agent Fuller, I have a suggestion. Instead of standing on the sidelines while your men run amuck in my town, why don't you let me join forces with them and see if I can't give them a hand? I'm an accomplished motorcycle rider, and I'm even registered to run in the race. I've lived in this area all of my life and know it like the back of my hand. And, if I do say so myself, I'm a damn good cop, and *you* could use my help."

Fuller was impressed. She wasn't like the other local Sheriffs who could have cared less about the FBI stepping on their jurisdictional toes. She had moxie, and Fuller liked moxie.

"You've got yourself a deal, Sheriff Nolan, but you will be working with one of my top agents. Just remember that he's in charge."

"No problem."

"Okay then, Connor O'Reilly is the agent on the case, and he will be in touch with you when he's got everything set up."

"Okay and thank you, Agent Fuller." Dallas placed the receiver back in its cradle, leaned back in her chair, and sighed.

Jesus H. Christ. What'd I do that for?

CHAPTER 5

THE DAY BEFORE the start of the race saw all the participants fine-tuning their motorcycles for the following morning's start.

Grams was no exception. She had spent the last week up to her armpits in grease and motorcycle parts, trying to get her bike ready. She told Dallas just that morning that it was "running like a finely tuned clock". Dallas thought, *Yeah, more like Big Ben,* because every time Grams started up the Indian, it rattled the windows in the house.

Yeah, some clock.

Dallas ducked her head in embarrassment when Grams decided to take her motorcycle to the compound. The ugly rattle of exhaust, the big blue puff of smoke, and the loud bang captured everyone's attention.

Crap, this is all I needed, Dallas thought. *I'm supposed to be here undercover, and I'm sticking out like a sore thumb.*

"Purrs like a kitten, don't you think, Dallas?"

"Yeah, like a saber tooth tiger."

Looking towards the sky, Dallas muttered, "God, give me strength."

Dallas knew her bike was as well tuned as she could get it, so she took full advantage of the free time to question fellow riders and their crew as to who was the person to beat. At least that was how she made her inquiries sound.

Agent Fuller had called to advise that her contact, Connor O'Reilly, would get in touch with her before the race started. The information that had been forwarded to Dallas from the Bureau had outlined the MO of the "Heirloom Bandit" – a name the news had given the perp. His robberies always seemed to correspond with special event motorcycle races. Apparently, wherever these races took place, homes of the wealthy residents were burglarized and fabulous family heirlooms were taken.

Agent Fuller had also given her a sketchy description of the suspect provided to the FBI by an overwrought elderly gentleman who had happened upon the thief and somehow, in the ensuing struggle, managed to partially unmask him. Fuller was not entirely convinced that the description was valid given the victim's state of mind and the fact that his eyesight was failing, but it was all they had to go on for now.

It was apparent this guy was a pro. He never left fingerprints, and the only person who had the opportunity to eyeball him was their slightly eccentric, upset old man. Fuller had told her about the strange mark the gentleman had noticed around the right side of the perp's collar bone, a tattoo possibly, not much bigger than a quarter.

How was she supposed to find that little mark? Smile pretty and say, "Strip please"?

Her questions to the other riders would give her the advantage of knowing some of the competition before the race began, and it wouldn't hurt in weeding out possible suspects either.

Her enquiries were innocent enough. In fact, to most she sounded more like a biker groupie than a rider and nothing at all like the law. Being tall, well built, and sexy as hell also went a long way in loosening up tongues.

Racers and their crews were normally closed mouth individuals, but with Dallas, they seemed eager to brag. They told her everything she wanted to know about the bikes and their riders, taking it for granted that she was more interested in being an ornament on the back of someone's powerful machine rather than the rider of one.

Leaving the concession area to a chorus of catcalls and whistles, Dallas strolled toward the area designated for riders to set up. Sleuthing aside, Dallas was also competitive. She hated to lose, and since she was in this race to test her riding abilities as well as her detective work, it didn't hurt to know who she was up against.

So far, she was pretty sure she had a good chance against most of the other riders. It stood to reason that she would have the advantage, since she had grown up in Colorado and ridden the back roads whenever she had the chance. Some of these guys were from the flatlands and were used to sand dunes, not cliffs that overlooked nothing but trees, trees, and more trees. From all accounts, her biggest challenge would be her FBI contact, Connor O'Reilly.

Hmm…way to remain inconspicuous.

Bent on finding out all she could about Agent O'Reilly, she sauntered into the area where the teams were setting up their trailers and getting ready for the race. Motorcycle engine parts and tires littered the ground, creating a maze that led Dallas' eye to the brand-new BMW G650 Sertao. Her mouth watered at the sight of BMW's newest state-of-the-art bike. Man, would she love to ride that in tomorrow's start. Unfortunately, she would have to make due with her five-year-old finely tuned Yamaha TW200. She knew it was in excellent running condition despite its age because she did all her own repairs.

Walking slowly toward the beautiful blue and white bike she appreciated its sleek lines and gleaming chrome.

Then, she noticed the man sitting on the ground working on the wheel hub. He was so engrossed in what he was doing that he didn't know Dallas was even there. This gave her a chance to observe the man closely. Walking up to the bike she purred, "Hi handsome, nice bike." Her voice was soft, sexy, and saccharine sweet.

The provocative voice penetrated Connor's concentration. It was pure sex, and it effectively caught his attention. Connor raised his head and looked through the spokes of the wheel at the most amazing pair of legs he had ever seen. Well shaped and beautifully tanned, they continued above the range of his vision. Wanting more, he moved his gaze upward until he was looking over the fender.

The legs seemed to go on forever, disappearing into the bottom of the shortest pair of shorts he had ever seen. Enjoying the view, he took his time and traveled up her body, coming to a waist so tiny he figured he could span it with his hands. The material of her shorts accentuated her waist and molded to her well-shaped derrière.

Her breasts were generous, the way he liked them. Well formed. The tanned skin above the tank top she wore tempted him to touch them. He just knew they would be as soft as down and would respond to the gentle touch of his hand and mouth.

He marveled that his intense scrutiny caused her nipples to turn into tight little buds that pressed erotically against the material of her barely-there tank top.

Connor could also feel the effect this little game was having on him. His jeans had suddenly become uncomfortably tight. So far hers was a body that even a blind man could savor.

Her green eyes gazed down at him; they were soft and seeming to feel the effects of sudden desire. Her tongue slipped between her full, pouting lips, seductively moistening the top one. Even if she hadn't been the most gorgeous thing he had seen in his life, that action alone would have been his undoing.

Maybe tonight won't be boring after all, he thought.

Connor wasn't sure he could stand up without embarrassing himself, but he knew he couldn't remain on the ground staring up at her like a befuddled school boy. Shifting his body so that the motorcycle would partially cover his arousal, he got to his feet.

Now that he was standing in front of her, Dallas couldn't believe her eyes. *Oh my God. It's him. The guy on the Harley.*

She was suddenly worried that he would recognize her – *the idiot* who had wrecked his Harley.

No wait, he hadn't seen her face because she hadn't taken off her helmet. Now some would think that confronting the man who wanted your head would rattle a person, but when you had to deal with the likes of Mrs. Ruttabaker and her exploits with her long dead husband, you quickly learned how to adapt.

But that was as far as her train of thought went. No man had ever looked at her the way this one was. She felt like she had been stripped naked and ravished, and he hadn't even laid a hand on her. The most unnerving thing was…she was enjoying every minute.

Pulling herself together, she leaned slightly forward, exposing more of her cleavage as she trailed her finger down the seat of the bike. She still had to find out who he was.

"Maybe you'd like to take me for a ride. I just love the feel of power between my legs."

Yeah, I'd like to take you for a ride, honey, but not on my bike, Connor thought to himself. She was…delicious.

"Maybe some other time, Red. Right now, I've got a race to get ready for."

"Oh, are you like one of the riders?" She put on her best bimbo speak.

"Why, are you looking for something to ride?"

"Yah. I was looking for Connor O'Reilly."

Dallas forced a girlish giggle knowing what that statement implied and playing on the effect it would have on him.

"I didn't mean it that way. I just want to see Connor. One of the guys down the way said I could find him here."

"Oh, are you a friend of O'Reilly's?" Connor asked. He was interested to know what her answer would be.

"Yah, we've been friends for like years. I wanted to give him a kiss for luck in the race. Isn't he like the best racer ever?" Dallas said, hoping this guy would give her some inside scoop on the mysterious Mr. O'Reilly.

"Well, O'Reilly's good, but I'm better. Why don't you give me that good luck kiss?"

Connor walked around the bike, grabbed her hands, and brought them around behind her back, effectively pinning her against his chest. He started to lower his head.

His face filled her vision. All Dallas could think was what his full sensuous lips would feel like pressed to hers; his tongue delving deep in her mouth and tongues twining.

Dallas started to panic.

Struggling against his vise-like grip was getting her nowhere. Without thinking, she hauled off and kicked him in the shin. Connor let out a string of curses and released her so he could rub his leg.

I don't know what your game is woman, but I sure as hell intend to find out.

This lady would never be a friend of his.

Gritting his teeth Connor growled, "I guess a quickie in my trailer is out of the question, so if there is nothing else I can do for you, I hope you'll excuse me."

"No wait! I need to talk to Connor...wish him luck..." Dallas stammered not realizing that she was closer to him than she knew.

"Lady, you just did all the talking to me that I can handle for one day. I don't know what your game is, but as far as I'm concerned, we're done. Go find some other sucker to play with."

And with that, he turned on his heel and walked to his trailer, closing the door behind him.

Dallas didn't know whether to crawl in a hole or slap him across the face. She knew she should have been a little less forward because he was the guy on the Harley she had cut off, but had he just admitted that he was Connor O' Reilly, her FBI contact?

Reality hit like a ton of bricks.

Oh crap! It's him – my contact. Well Dallas, you just blew it. Good detective work Sheriff Dumb and Dumber.

Eyeing his bike once again she just couldn't help touching the gleaming metal. Dallas trailed her hand lightly over the bike to the handlebars and then ran it over the soft kid leather of the seat. She was tempted to mount the bike but wanted to mount the rider even more.

Get a grip, Dallas.

Heaving a sigh, she turned away, wistfully glancing back at what she wished was hers – and she wasn't thinking about the bike.

Dallas turned again and walked away.

CHAPTER 6

CONNOR WAS LOOKING over the FBI files on the burglaries when the door to the trailer opened.

Maybe the redhead has changed her mind and come back to finish what she started.

The thought of that had his heart beating a hopeful tattoo against his chest. His reaction to her had bothered him. He was not one to let a woman, no matter how good looking, get under his skin.

Much to Connor's disappointment though, it was J.T. who walked through the door. He sauntered over to the mini-fridge and pulled out a beer.

"Are you finished tinkering with the bike?" J.T. asked as he pulled the tab on the can.

"Yeah, I decided to go with the mousse tires after all. Just finished putting them on. I figured there is no sense in carrying more equipment than I have to."

"Good thinking. Changing a flat on the course can cost valuable time. At least with the mousse tires, you can run to the next checkpoint. Wanna beer?"

"No thanks," Connor said. "I don't need the morning-after head."

"Okay, as soon as I finish my beer, I'll take the bike to the impound area," J.T. volunteered.

Connor nodded his head in agreement. All the motorcycles were locked up overnight in an impound area in order to prevent cheating. There were only certain parts that could be replaced after the race had started; the others were marked so that any tampering would be immediately noticed.

Still riders tried to cheat – even to the extent of switching bikes.

"What's up buddy? You seem distracted. Tough case, or are you bothered about start day tomorrow? I know it's rough terrain, but you've ridden harder."

J.T. knew the problem on Connor's mind wasn't the race; Con had filled him in on the burglaries. J.T knew the local law was to be involved in the investigation and that meant Connor was supposed to initiate contact. He also knew Connor was in for a surprise in that area.

Connor hadn't had enough time when he reached Desire to check in with the local sheriff. After his run in with the idiot that had cut him off, he had only enough time to confirm his registration and find out where to set up his trailer. After that, he had decided to do a little investigating on his own before he talked to the local law.

J.T. knew when Connor found out that Dallas Nolan was not only number one on his shit list but also the Sheriff of Desire, he would be furious with J.T. for not filling him in sooner.

Staring at the course layout, Connor said in answer to J.T.'s question: "Some of the course is downright deadly, but that's not what's got my goat. It's the case. How can something that appears so simple to solve on paper be so damn convoluted?"

He wasn't really asking, just talking out loud. Connor had decided he wasn't going to talk about the redhead who had just visited him, even to J.T. His friend knew him almost as well as Connor knew himself, and he would guess right off the effect the redhead had on him.

"No case is ever simple; you know that. What else is bothering you?" J.T. pushed a little harder.

"Well, some ditsy redhead was hanging around here claiming to know me and wanting to wish me luck. She was up to something, but we never got past the sexual innuendos to find out what that something was," Connor reluctantly admitted.

"Sexual innuendos? Hmm...I think maybe you got yourself all hot and bothered by this woman, and now you're looking for things that just aren't there. She's probably someone's biker-babe, and she was just looking for an advantage...or looking for a good time."

J.T. knew without asking who the redhead was. Dallas was checking out the competition by using her looks to her advantage, but she was probably also getting a jump on the case and looking for a suspect.

Sneaky but effective. J.T. knew this lady would give Connor a run for his money both in the race and in the investigation.

"Yeah, she was a looker alright, but I don't like liars, and she was up to no-good," Connor fumed.

Not bothering to comment, J.T. finished his beer and tossed the can in the trash. "Time to call it a night," he said, muffling a yawn. "Get some rest, Connor. Don't worry about the race, and don't worry about the girl."

"Yeah, right."

Connor knew it would take more than J.T.'s encouragement to get that body out of his mind. Shutting off the light, he crawled into his bunk. Connor knew that he wouldn't be able to relax.

Her face, framed by a cloud of flame-red hair, floated around in his mind. Green eyes beckoned him to come to her. The thought of her naked body aroused him. After tossing and turning for what seemed like hours, Connor got out of bed and paced. But pacing did nothing to alleviate his condition – a cold shower was what he needed. He didn't bother with any hot water at all; he just let the cold water pelt him back into reality.

This woman had all the warnings of trouble with a capital 'T'.

DALLAS COULDN'T BELIEVE what she had done. At the time, it felt so right, but she now felt entirely stupid – embarrassed even. Of all the dumb-ass, unprofessional things to do. All that time, she had been making a fool of herself by saying she was a friend of Connor O'Reilly, when she was actually talking to the man. Just the thought of how stupid she must have sounded to him made her stomach flip. The fact that he was her FBI contact only compounded her dim-witted feeling.

Stupid, stupid, stupid.

When he learned that *she* was the rider that had mowed him down at the intersection, what would he think? Even worse, would be him finding out that *she* was the Dallas Nolan that never showed up at the Sheriff's office to square up with him. But the ultimate humiliation would be when he learned that *she* was the town Sheriff, and worse still – if that was even possible – that *she* was his local contact for trying to find out who their perpetrator was.

He was going to blow a gasket clear to Pueblo.

Dallas berated herself for how foolish she must have appeared to him. How would he ever take her seriously as a law-enforcement agent now?

She remembered how uncomfortable she had felt when he literally undressed her with his eyes, how absolutely humiliated she felt when she realized who he was, and how incredibly turned on she was when he pinned her to his body. Remembering the power of his extremely muscled chest pressed up against her breasts, the strength in his arms as he pulled her up against his length, and the pulsing of his arousal against her stomach had her heart thumping like a bass drum.

Dallas always tried to have the upper hand in any situation, but tonight she had gotten a taste of what it was like to be on the other side – a taste of something wild and passionate, something *way* beyond her control. She could still feel his breath on her face. She still remembered the anticipation of the kiss that never came.

Her musing came to a halt when she heard a knock at the door to her trailer. Secretly, she hoped that somehow Connor had come to finish what they had started. Arousal hit her deep and hard – again, but that was soon knocked out of her when she heard Grams screech, "I'll get it, dear."

Dallas had almost forgotten that Grams was in the trailer with her. She'd been quiet for a change…practicing her yoga. Dallas had always found it hysterical to watch Grams try to contort her arthritic joints into directions they were never meant to go – not even in her youth. Her yoga getups were even more bewildering; they were enough to give you vertigo.

How anyone could find peace wearing chartreuse paisley tights was beyond her.

"That's okay, Grams. I'll get it." Dallas figured it would take Grams a few minutes to unravel herself anyway.

She didn't realize that she had been holding her breath until she opened the door and saw J.T. standing there. She tried not to let her disappointment show. She forced a smile and said, a little too cheerfully, "What a nice surprise."

Holy redhead, Batman! was the only thing that J.T. could think of as he stared at the sensuous creature before him. Clearing his throat and trying not to swallow his tongue, J.T. stammered, "Hey Dallas. Just wanted to drop by and wish you good luck for tomorrow. I certainly hope you get what you want out of this race."

And maybe a little something you weren't expecting.

"That's very sweet of you, J.T. Would you like to come in for coffee?" she asked, more out of politeness than enthusiasm for his company. What she really wanted was for him to go away so she could daydream some more about Connor O'Reilly and the feelings he had aroused in her.

"Well, hello there, Jeremy Theodore," Grams greeted J.T.

"Little late for a social call, son."

J.T. COULDN'T STOP his jaw from dropping. Just when he thought he had seen it all, here was Grandma Nolan decked out in a skin-tight, two-piece, god-awful, green paisley costume. And man, it was tight. No woman in her right mind and who had lost her fight with gravity would be caught dead wearing it.

C. G. SALO

But then again, Grandma Nolan was in a league of her own.

"Hi Grams. I'm not staying." Turning to Dallas, he said, "Thanks for the offer of coffee, but I'd better be going. It's been a long day. Just wanted to wish you luck."

J.T. backed away from Dallas' door and into the path of another rider.

"Sorry man, didn't see you coming."

The man just nodded in acknowledgment, his eyes widening when he caught sight of Dallas standing in the doorway. A knowing smirk came over his face. He was wrongly assuming that J.T. just had finished a little recreational activity before tomorrow's race.

J.T. did not miss the look and did not much like what the look implied. Waving goodnight to Dallas, he turned and gave a slight nod of his head in the man's direction.

Alex Cross hesitated a moment before entering his trailer. If there was one thing he always appreciated, it was a beautiful woman. Looking over his shoulder at Dallas' trailer, he thought, *Man, would I ever like a piece of that action.*

CONNOR WASN'T THE only person Dallas had questioned that day. She had already sent the list of riders participating in this NSDE to Betty, the only person she trusted to conduct computer searches on her suspects. Dallas was especially interested in the ones that she had her "gut" feeling about.

She knew she wasn't going to get to sleep any time soon, so she settled at the small Formica-covered counter that served as a table. Grams had already taken herself off to bed, saying she needed her beauty sleep, so she was confident she wouldn't be interrupted.

Betty had Jim Bobbin, one of her deputies, drop off the rap sheets she had pulled. After skimming over the highlights on each one, Dallas focused on the two men that had tweaked her interest.

Frank Morelli, a rider from New Jersey, was the first. He had a very interesting and very in-depth arrest jacket. Seems Mr. Morelli had been very busy as a young boy, and an even busier adult, the rap sheet was three pages long and documented criminal activity that ranged from shop lifting as an adolescent to grand theft auto as recently as two years ago. What bothered Dallas was that there were no arrests or convictions since that time. Either he had gotten smarter and not been caught, or he had straightened out his act. Whatever the case, the timeframe for some of the robberies fit.

But it was the second profile that had her twitching. On the surface, there was no valid reason for it. There wasn't even cause for a second look.

Other than fitting the physical description given by the victim in Texas, Mr. Alex Cross' criminal record was all but nonexistent. The only trouble he had ever been in was in his late teens when he had been picked up on suspicion of B&E, but he was later released because the charges were dropped.

Since then, he hadn't even had a parking violation.

Dallas pushed the file away and leaned back, closing her eyes. Fatigue must have her seeing things that just weren't there.

No, it was more than that. Something about the person listed on paper tripped her switches. Tomorrow before the race, she would call Betty and ask her to dig deeper on both men. In the meantime, she would keep a close eye on them during the race.

Dallas was drained. She was so tired she couldn't focus on the words written on the rap sheets. She figured she'd fall asleep the minute her head hit the pillow, but that wasn't the case. Left to her own thoughts, in the quiet of her room, they returned to Connor O'Reilly.

The bloody nerve of him leading her on that way and then treating her like a sex toy. Of course, she had conveniently forgotten that she had been dressed like someone's plaything *and* had instigated the encounter.

She still found it hard to believe that he was her FBI contact. She had been expecting a non-descript, stereotypical, bland kind of guy – not a man with a body and face that would stop traffic.

CONNOR HAD SPENT his night much as Dallas had. Sleep was a long time coming for both Dallas and Connor. Both awoke feeling that they had been dragged through a mud hole backwards.

Getting psyched for the day's race was going to take a lot of hot coffee.

CHAPTER 7

EVEN SUFFERING FROM sleep deprivation, Connor was stoked about the race. The anticipation, the noise, and the nervous energy combined to give him a high that no drug known to man could match. The only thing that added a sour note were the headlines in the morning paper screaming: **The Heirloom Bandit strikes again.**

They hadn't even begun their investigation into this thief, and he had pulled off another heist.

The story claimed that the night before someone had ripped off the house of a local businessman while he was out of town. Several antique pieces were taken; pieces that had been in his family for over one hundred years.

The Heirloom Bandit was nothing if not consistent. He rarely took anything common. He took items that held more than monetary value. These were pieces that held strong historical value – pieces that would be hard to replace by insurance settlements. Connor crumpled up the paper and threw it on the table.

Damn it. He hadn't even started his investigation and already he was one step behind.

THE DAY WAS starting out bright and sunny and not too hot – good conditions for racing, but it didn't help Connor's sudden black mood. He was pissed that this guy had gotten the jump on them, but he didn't have time to think about it now; the racers were beginning to line up for the start of the race.

The smell of the gasoline igniting in the powerful engines, the sound of tires peeling out, and the camaraderie that would soon change to aggressive competition at the sound of the starter's pistol filled the air. Connor was in his element. He had drawn the fourth-place start time. Not bad.

Start times were chosen by random selection, each rider going off at one-minute intervals. The riders' departure time for the start of each day's race was marked on their time card. The judges had already calculated the time it should take to arrive at each checkpoint when travelling at a pre-determined speed. This speed was defined by the terrain and risk of each leg of the race. A faster time was always good – it meant that you had a little extra time to give your bike a rest, refuel, or if something was broken, to fix it without worrying about a major time loss. That didn't mean you could be overly cautious on each leg of the race though. A disqualifying time was also built into the pre-set time. It could be as little as fifteen minutes over or as much as forty-five minutes over, depending on the day's racing conditions. Arriving at the checkpoints one minute over that time was an automatic disqualification.

As each rider crossed the designated checkpoints, their actual time was recorded. The difference between this time and the calculated time dictated how long they would have for allowed procedures at each checkpoint.

Some checkpoints gave them time to refuel and service

their bikes; others did not. If a rider came in way behind schedule, he might only have time to refuel, and any mechanical adjustments would have to wait. This was all part of the excitement and the challenge of the NSDE.

Connor knew his bike was in top running condition. He had just finished fine tuning it when "Red" had interrupted him. Just the thought of her had his emotions in an uproar. Anger at her lying to him mixed with lust at remembering her lush body crushed against his. Conner mentally slapped himself. This was not where he wanted his thoughts to go just before race time.

Over the P.A. system Connor heard the first five starters called to the line. Dallas Nolan was one of them.

Connor's features hardened at the sound of his name. "Looks like I'll get my chance to even the score with the asshole who wrecked my Harley."

As his mechanic, J.T. was allowed to be at the start line with Connor.

"When I get my hands on that guy, I'm going to make him wish he was never born," Connor barked at J.T.

"Don't think about it right now, Con. You have more important things to think about."

J.T. knew full well who it was that Connor was speaking about.

"Yeah, you're right. You gonna wish me luck?"

"What the hell for? You know you're the best there is. Is that enough ego stroking for you?" J.T. said.

"Smart ass," Connor growled.

Dallas was having similar thoughts. Excitement threaded through her as she suited up. The thrill of the race, coupled with all the information she had gathered the day before, had Dallas feeling she had a slight edge over both the other racers and one FBI agent. This fueled her confidence.

Standing on the sidelines she surveyed her competitors. Some she recognized, including Grandma Nolan in her tattered lemon-yellow riding leathers. Others she didn't. But the one that stood out was Connor O'Reilly. Her body betrayed her yet again. Just when she should be feeling anger over his treatment of her, it was desire that coursed through her. Tall and muscular, he caused her heart to...

Dallas gave herself a mental shake. *Focus, focus, focus* was the mantra that repeated in her head. Slamming down the visor on her helmet and giving her gloves a final tug, she revved the engine and headed off toward the starting line just as her name was called for the first five starters.

Looking down the line of riders, Dallas felt adrenaline surge through her veins. Frowning, she knew the next six days were going to be taxing, not only because of the race, but also because of the investigation. Pushing all negative thoughts to the back of her mind, she mentally went over the route for today's run. Because she was very familiar with this first day's course, she visualized the points at which she could safely make her moves on any of the other riders.

She noticed that Connor had a good start. Dallas knew she would have to get a jump on him if she was going to win the first leg of the competition. She revved her engine in anticipation.

Suddenly, the air was shattered by a loud bang. People dove for cover.

Dallas looked down the line of riders only to see Grandma Nolan, or more accurately the spot where Grandma Nolan was supposed to be, filled with a cloud of black smoke. A tiny figure emerged from the cloud coughing up a storm and cursing a blue streak.

Dallas didn't have time to go over and check on her grandmother because she was signaled to go. She glanced briefly at her grandmother, who was being escorted off the track, and selfishly felt comforted knowing she would have one less thing to worry about now.

CHAPTER 8

THE FIRST LEG of the race was one of the most demanding Conner had ever run. The layout was not going to be kind to man let alone machine. Ten miles into the race, they were off the dirt road and into a rock-strewn glacial cut. Ruts the size of the Grand Canyon threatened to throw rider and bike off the many cliffs that rose up in their path, and the next twenty miles were all uphill.

Concentration and skill were paramount.

In an effort to stay ahead of the pack, Connor almost lost control a few times. Having to constantly check his speed was going to cost him time on his day's run. The only consolation was that everyone else would be in the same boat. Not willing to throw caution completely to the wind, he did pick up the pace a little.

Nothing can prepare a person for their first glimpse of the monstrous Rockies. Even from a distance, their greatness seems powerful and perhaps even somewhat overwhelming. Dallas shivered knowing that soon she would be enveloped in their embrace. Exhilaration coursed through her. She had the distinct feeling that she had been here before. Not on one her many rides through the area, but in the past.

Maybe it was the lure of ancient voices; whispers on the wind in the vast forest that encompassed this state. If you listened hard enough, you could almost hear the war cries of the tribes that once roamed this majestic land or the voices of the settlers who came here claiming it for their own. Both tried desperately not to interfere with Mother Nature and her beautiful bounty.

Dallas always felt like she was coming home when she rode through the area. The grandeur of the Rockies always made her feel small and insignificant. These mountains had a long history of swallowing up the weak or making heroes out of the strong.

She had often been told that she was a strong person. Things that would put normal people on the verge of a heart attack barely had her breathing hard. It was this strength that had Dallas pushing herself almost to the point of recklessness to try and gain ground on O'Reilly. She knew trying to put that man out of her mind was useless. His face floated on the edges of her thoughts: handsome yet rugged, a smile playing the corners of his sensuous mouth. Broad shoulders, bulging biceps, arms reaching for...

Sudden pain shot up from Dallas' toes to her jaw, jarring her from her daydream. "What the...?" was all she could say as she fought to bring the bike under control. The rear tire slid on the loose dirt and gravel, tilting the bike dangerously close to a wipe out. Gearing down and braking gently, she managed to stop.

Heart pounding, she looked back at the four-foot drop she had just come off. Concerned for the bike, she stopped and checked it thoroughly. To her immense relief everything seemed to be okay.

"Damn it!" she chided herself out loud.

Her aching jaw would be enough to keep her mind on the race from this point on.

Catching sight of a rider through a stand of trees, Dallas taxed her bike to the limit in an effort to close the gap between them. Finally close enough, she realized that this was not O'Reilly but rider number three. *Crap! Where the hell was he?*

Her bike was straining under the arduous pace she was putting it through in her effort to overtake Connor. Catching up to rider number three and leaving him behind was not easy, but Dallas managed to accomplish it, effectively putting enough distance between them that she was confident he would not be able to overtake her.

Just when she had resigned herself to finishing under her time but behind Connor, she caught a fleeting glimpse of him as he rode through an outcrop of granite. Spotting what she knew was a shortcut, she decided to ride over the outcrop. She knew that this maneuver would have her catching air for the second time today, but this time she would be expecting it.

Timing her approach and executing a perfect jump, she not only caught up to Connor, but effectively cut him off – again. That hadn't been her intention, but it worked. Dallas was now in the lead.

Giving a wave of triumph, she felt confident enough to back off on her speed, giving her bike a well-deserved breather.

Son of a bitch. Not again!

Connor was furious. The time he had made up on rider number three he had just lost to Nolan. No one could be stupid enough to cut him off a second time and think they would live to tell about it.

Nolan, you're mine.

Connor was gaining ground, but as he neared Dallas, his engine started to misfire.

Now what?

Easing off on the throttle didn't resolve the problem. Connor slipped into neutral and revved the engine a couple times. Still misfiring. This shouldn't be happening. Before going to impound, the bike was in perfect running condition. He had checked and rechecked everything before Red showed up. She couldn't have done anything to the bike. He was with her the whole time.

No, you weren't. You walked away and left her there...

Connor didn't like where this was going. He had no choice but to pull over. There were only two possibilities: No gas or loose spark plug cable.

The gas gauge registered three quarters full, so the only other alternative was the cable. Checking the spark plug proved him right. Someone knew just how much to lift the cable so that it wouldn't be noticed, but would rattle loose – especially over all this rough terrain.

Quickly securing the wire, Connor jumped back on his bike. Several riders had already passed him, so he knew he was going to have a hard time making up the loss. His focus now had to be on finishing the day without any more delay. *Then*, he would concentrate on how he was going to punish Dallas Nolan and his redheaded accomplice.

Connor didn't catch a glimpse of Nolan for the remainder of the course – not until the last checkpoint.

His ego took a beating when he realized how far down the list he had finished. It was lower than he had ever finished before. Connor had *never* come in lower than third place – not even in his very first race.

To make matters even worse, if that were possible, the jerk who had cut him off was being congratulated by everyone for obviously placing first in this heat. White rage flashed through him as he charged towards the group, hell-bent on having the distinct pleasure of decking the guy.

His eyes narrowed as he approached, and then opened wide in shock. The scene unfolding in front of him seemed to move in slow motion. He watched the rider's hands come up and remove his helmet. In one fluid motion, the helmet came off and with a shake of *her* head, Dallas' lustrous flame-red hair cascaded down her back. Several shorter curls framed her face. A smile of triumph played around her luscious lips.

Connor stopped dead in his tracks. His anger was replaced with surprise, and all rational thought vanished except one: Dallas Nolan was a woman!

Not only was he a she, but the same she that had enticed him at his trailer the night before.

"What the hell happened to you Connor?" J.T. said as he pushed his way through the crowd around the riders. He was stunned and concerned. He had never known Connor to place this poorly in a race before.

Connor just stared dumbfounded at Dallas. He turned on J.T. "You knew all along, didn't you?" he yelled.

"Knew what?" J.T. replied.

"That she was a woman."

"That who was a woman? What the hell are you talking about?"

J.T. was slightly confused until he caught the direction in which Connor was glaring.

"Oh!"

"Oh? Oh? Is that all you can say? That woman is a menace. Not only that, she sabotaged my bike. I'm gonna strangle her with my bare hands. I don't care if she is a woman."

"Whoa! Hold on a minute. What do you mean 'sabotaged your bike'?"

"She sabotaged my bike. She pulled the spark-plug cable. She was, she was..."

Connor was livid.

J.T. couldn't believe what he was hearing. He knew Dallas would never do what Conner was accusing her of. She was a Sheriff, for crying out loud!

"You've got to be kidding. Why the hell would she do something like that?"

"I don't know, but I'm sure as hell going to find out."

Turning away from J.T., Connor charged over to where everyone was congratulating Dallas. J.T. ran after him, caught him by the arm, and spun him around. "You can't barge in there, accusing her of something that you have no proof of."

"Watch me." Connor wasn't about to listen to reason. He was going to see this woman pay, one way or the other.

J.T. wasn't sure what he could do for Dallas at this point. She had gotten herself into this pickle, so J.T. beat a hasty retreat. He decided to seek higher ground to avoid the line of fire but still have the advantage of watching the fireworks. *Connor didn't realize who he was going up against.* Just the thought had J.T.'s shoulders shaking with laughter.

Dallas was no shrinking violet, and she would give as good as she got.

Connor's fury was evident as he made his way toward her and the little band of groupies. Shouldering his way through the crowd of well wishers, he came up behind Dallas, grabbed her shoulder, and spun her around.

"You little bitch."

Taken completely by surprise, Dallas could only stare at Connor in shock.

"Did you really think you could get away with it?"

"With..."

"That took a lot of balls."

"What?"

"Do you know what they would do if I turned you in to the officials? They would dump your ass. No one likes a cheat."

"Who..."

"Using your looks and your body to try to gain an advantage over the other riders."

"You ass..."

"You are the lowest, most conniving, despicable excuse for a woman I have ever run into, and trust me, babe, I've met a few."

Dallas was dumbfounded. Some of the riders were beginning to whisper. *You arrogant jerk,* she thought. She couldn't get a word in edgewise, so she did the only other thing she could think of to shut Connor up. She punched him right on the jaw, then turned and stormed away.

Dallas kept both fists clenched at her sides. Tears pricked

the backs of her eyelids. She would be damned before she would let anyone know just how much her hand hurt from that punch.

Connor was so shocked he couldn't speak. Rubbing his jaw, he thought, *Man, she packs a wallop!*

J.T. was doubled over with laughter. This was better than any soap opera on TV. He could hardly wait to see the next episode.

"Connor," J.T. said, choking on his laughter, "do you know what you just did? You just insulted your 'local yokel' contact. That's Sheriff Dallas Nolan, and she's supposed to be your partner in trying to catch your thief."

Connor stared at J.T. in shocked silence. Then he did what he knew would make him feel better for the moment but terrible later on: He hauled off and slammed a meaty fist into J.T.'s jaw.

His friend went flying backward, landing on his ass. He was still laughing like a hyena.

Connor's fist throbbed. J.T.'s jaw was stronger than it looked.

CHAPTER 9

LATER THAT EVENING, Dallas, J.T., and a few other riders were enjoying burgers and beer in a local diner when Connor entered. Dallas immediately noticed the change on J.T.'s face. It was as if the devil had just picked him to do a favor. She turned around to see who had entered the pub.

It was O'Reilly.

She had wondered how J.T. had come by the bruise on his jaw, now she knew.

J.T. hastily whispered, "Get the hell out of here."

She hesitated for a second, not wanting to look like a coward. Then she took his advice and retreated to the ladies' room, hoping to avoid another confrontation.

If she thought O'Reilly was angry at their first encounter, he looked downright in league with the devil right now.

"Now, Connor..." J.T. never had a chance to finish his cautionary sentence.

"Shut up J.T. Just shut the hell up," hissed a furious Connor. His face, marred by a colorful bruise, was a mask of cold rage accompanied by a wicked smile that spoke volumes.

"I'm going to enjoy this."

J.T. prayed that there was a back door for Dallas' sake. He

didn't bother chasing after him. He knew Connor would never do anything physical to her – at least not physically painful. He just needed to vent.

Everyone had known who Dallas was before Connor did and that irked Connor O'Reilly, "FBI agent extraordinaire", to no end.

He didn't hesitate as he stormed after Dallas. He followed her right into the ladies' room, never once considering or caring that there could be other women in there doing their thing.

Dallas whirled around to face her adversary and came nose to nose with him as he proceeded to back her into a wall.

"What the hell do you think you are doing following me in here? Didn't we already go through all of this macho man routine?"

Dallas *was* disappointed to find no back door – not even a window to open and crawl out of. *Coward,* she whispered to herself.

"Woman, we haven't even begun to go through this!" Connor snarled.

"The way I see it, you owe me five thousand dollars and one hell of an apology for wrecking my Harley and an explanation about why you ditched me back in Desire and what the hell was up with the horny vamp act yesterday."

Dallas was incensed, mostly because he was right on all counts. *Damn,* she hated it when someone had the upper hand.

"I'll pay you the money for your bike."

She decided that first mark against her was the easiest for her to fix; she would find the money somewhere. Hopefully, he wouldn't expect anything more right at the moment.

Connor wasn't expecting her to acquiesce so quickly. He needed to get in one more jab.

"And not only that, but of all the low-down sneaky things to do – tampering with another rider's bike during a race is tantamount to…to…"

"I have no idea what you are talking about," she countered with hands on hips. "When would I have had an opportunity to do such a thing? You were with me the whole time. How could I have tampered with anything?"

"I saw you touching my ride before you walked away yesterday. You're the only possible suspect. No one else with integrity would ever dream up a scheme to disable another rider's motorcycle."

Connor was glaring down at her. "Just like a woman to try something underhanded. Did it give you some kind of a rush?"

Dallas did a very good job of hiding just how much his words were affecting her. Masking her confusion, she yelled right back at him. "How dare you accuse me of cheating? I didn't do anything to your stupid bike."

She pulled herself up to her full five foot eight inches and practically hissed at him, "You were there the whole time. There is no possible way that I could have tampered with your bike. Besides, you rode that course today. You know it was filled with enough ruts and bumps to shake anything loose."

Not feeling as confident as she looked, she tried to push past him. "Now if you don't mind, O'Reilly, get out and leave me alone. And try to act like a man, not a macho idiot!"

At that precise moment, Connor realized why it was that this woman distracted him so much. Even in the throes of anger, this woman's beauty was electrifying. Those green eyes, ablaze with anger, could hypnotize a man. Her sun-bronzed skin with that little smatter of freckles across the bridge of her nose was appealing, but it was her full, sexy, kissable lips that were his undoing.

Connor grabbed her arms and pulled her up against his body. He just couldn't stop himself. He lowered his head to that sensuous mouth, even though he knew in the back of his mind that he was going to seriously regret what he was about to do.

But he did it anyway.

Dallas' eyes widened in shock when she realized that right in the middle of their diatribe, he was going to kiss her. She was positively mesmerized by the intensity of his eyes. They were as clear blue as a summer sky. She couldn't move, nor did she want to.

Her tongue involuntarily skimmed her suddenly dry lips, moistening them in anticipation of the kiss she knew was going to be explosive.

Eyes glazed with lust, Connor whispered as he grabbed her shoulders and pulled her to his chest. "We both want this."

Lips came together in a fusion of molten desire. Tongues entwined as passion built between them.

Dallas could feel his arms tighten around her, drawing them closer together, molding their bodies to each other. Desire wicked away the fires of anger between them. The kiss deepened. Passion flared.

Connor was the first to break away from the torrid embrace.

Without a word, he turned on his heel and walked out of the washroom, leaving Dallas standing there struggling to regain her composure and trying to comprehend the magnitude of what just happened.

She had just given herself over completely to Connor, and for that she was slightly disgusted with herself. But it comforted her to know that Connor seemed to have been as deeply affected by that kiss as she was.

J.T. was waiting outside of the ladies' room when Connor stormed out. He wasn't expecting the look of total confusion on his friend's face.

"What happened? Is she all right?"

"Yeah, she's all right."

"Why the hell are you so concerned about her anyway?" Connor demanded.

"Dallas is a friend."

"Really! I thought *I* was your friend. Why the hell didn't you just tell me from the start who she was?"

"Ah Con, you know how much I like a good laugh, and trust me, this has been the best one in a *long* time."

Then, for the second time that day, Connor hauled off and slugged his friend.

J.T. sat on the floor beside the ladies' room, rubbing his already aching jaw. He knew he deserved it, but in his own defense he said, "You know, Connor, if we *weren't* such good friends, I'd have to do something about this new habit of yours."

FROM HIS TABLE in a corner of the pub, Alex Cross watched the scene unfold between O'Reilly and the redhead. He always chose a spot where he could keep his back to the wall. Experience had taught him that.

He could only imagine what had just transpired behind the closed door of the ladies' room. But by the scowl on O'Reilly's face and the way he stormed out, it couldn't have been good.

Sizing up his competition helped him keep his edge, and this little confrontation had proved very interesting. Something about Connor O'Reilly bothered him. He couldn't quite put his finger on what it was, but he fully intended to keep his eye on him.

Alex had been just a little upset when the woman had made the first checkpoint in the first spot. He had figured that honor would have gone to him, not to some female. Picking up his drink, he went in search of more information on what exactly had gone down between them. Maybe he could use it to his advantage – maybe it could provide some entertainment.

After all, the woman was not bad to look at.

Walking casually toward the table where J.T. and his buddies sat, Alex strained to pick up the conversation. Maybe he could glean some tidbit with which to insinuate himself on them. As he came even with their table, J.T. burst out laughing and made some comment about Connor having finally met his match.

Alex used this as his opening. "So, what's with O'Reilly? Is he going soft on the redhead?" he asked as he pulled out a chair and made himself at home.

J.T. wasn't entirely fooled by Alex's interest. He felt that the man was up to something – especially after bumping into him outside Dallas' trailer. He didn't mind expanding on the not-so-subtle competition between Connor and Dallas, but he was not about to reveal their real motive for being involved with the race.

"So... Connor thinks the girl tampered with his bike."

"Yeah, but I'm not so sure. We were watching the area the whole time. Dallas never had an opportunity to sabotage anything...except for maybe his ego."

The mirror behind J.T.'s head showed Dallas exiting the ladies' bathroom. Alex waited until she was right behind them before he made his next comment.

"My God man, what's O'Reilly thinking? You said she's the local sheriff, for Pete's sake. She wouldn't jeopardize her position here." Alex shook his head. "No, I just can't believe that she would do something like that."

Dallas reached the table in time to hear Alex's last comment. After the scene that had just unfolded in the washroom, she didn't need the pat on the back, especially from Alex Cross, but she accepted it nonetheless.

"Thanks, but O'Reilly doesn't seem to agree with you... Alex, isn't it?" she said as she extended her hand towards him.

The fact that Alex fit the description of their suspect to a T hadn't escaped her notice.

Dallas pulled out the chair beside him. When she was seated, he asked her if she wanted a drink.

"Sure, a Perrier please. Have to keep a clear head for the race tomorrow."

After a half an hour of idle conversation, the rest of the racers excused themselves, as they needed their rest for the next day's start. This left Dallas and Alex alone at the table.

She couldn't shake the feeling that there might be more to Mr. Alex Cross than met the eye. She decided to use this opportunity to question him on his background, hoping she sounded casually interested and not like *Columbo*.

"So Alex, how long have you been racing?" Dallas forced herself to sound relaxed.

"A few years now – mostly motocross, but this is my second endurance race. What about you? I would think your duties as Sheriff would have left you with little time to compete in this race, considering it starts and ends in your town."

"I'm kinda like you. I like racing – mostly motocross. This is my first endurance race, and I'm liking it so far," she said trying to be totally evasive.

It didn't escape Alex's notice that Dallas hadn't exactly answered his question. That evasiveness made him wonder what she had to hide, but he didn't want to push his luck, so he decided not to squeeze her for any information on O'Reilly. He didn't want to sound obvious.

Trying to keep her talking a little longer, he asked, "What does O'Reilly say happened to his bike?"

"Oh, something about the spark plug cable coming loose."

"And he blames you for that? That's the lamest thing I've ever heard. You ran that course today. It was full of enough ruts and potholes to shake anything loose."

The fact that he had repeated her words to Connor verbatim made her wonder whether it was just coincidence or if he had been listening to their conversation.

"Yah, that's exactly what I told him." She kept her tone neutral, not wanting to alert him to her suspicions.

Dallas looked at her watch. "Look at the time. I guess we'd better get to bed."

Alex smiled at the thought. That was exactly where he intended to get her – but not tonight. Choosing not to respond to her faux pas, Alex walked Dallas to her trailer.

"Get a good night's sleep. We've got another tough day ahead of us tomorrow."

Alex stood outside his trailer door for a moment. He hadn't gotten what he wanted out of their conversation, but that didn't mean that he wouldn't keep plying her for more information. Alex figured that Sheriff Dallas Nolan was no threat to him, but he wasn't so sure about O'Reilly.

He had to figure out what his next step would be.

THERE WAS SOMEONE else who had more than a passing interest in the action at the pub that night. Frank Morelli had been seated at the far end of the bar, nursing his beer. He had chosen this vantage point because he could easily watch everyone who came in and see who they associated with and who they left with.

If nothing else, life had taught him to always know his surroundings, and there certainly were some interesting events unfolding in this race. His curiosity had been peaked by the obvious altercation between the tall dark-haired racer and the pretty redhead, but his lessons of life had also taught him never to get involved in things that were not his affair.

It had saved his life on more than one occasion, and he was not about to push his luck now. So, he had sat back and enjoyed the show.

CHAPTER 10

IT WAS DAY two of the race, and Dallas was more than a little worried. After her conversation with Alex Cross the previous night, she had called Betty to follow up on her suspicions about Cross and Morelli. Betty had told her that they both had some closed files, and it would take some "maneuvering" on Betty's part to open them.

For all that her receptionist looked, sounded, and acted like a flake, Betty was a computer genius, and she could work her way into any computer, anywhere. Dallas needed to give Betty some breathing room to work her magic, so she decided to focus on the race. She wasn't so sure that Connor wasn't going to pay her back for what he imagined was nefarious activity on her part, so she checked and re-checked her bike to reassure herself that he hadn't.

Everything seemed fine.

She had even scanned the papers that morning and noted that their Heirloom Bandit hadn't struck again. It seemed like he had very discerning tastes: He chose his targets carefully, and it would appear that this town held nothing that piqued his interest.

With this lack of activity on his part, Dallas decided she

would focus on the race today. Because her run the previous day had placed her in first, Dallas was now near the back of the pack to give the other racers a chance to improve their place in the standings. Waiting for her start gave her too much time to go over yesterday's events, and one thing that kept creeping into her mind was Connor's kiss.

She couldn't seem to remove it from her thoughts, and if she didn't, it was really going to screw up her day. She wouldn't be able to concentrate on the race or tracking down her suspects if she kept thinking about it. The starter's horn cut off any other musings about Connor, their kiss, or any other physical encounter with him.

One by one, the riders took off. It looked like it would be a good day's run. The weather was still holding with beautiful, sunny skies, a comfortable temperature, and a slight breeze. If it continued, each rider could be assured of running a good time.

Connor was one of those riders. He had a feeling that today would be fruitful for him. He had double-checked his bike for any tampering, and it came up clean. Clearing his mind of any distractions, especially thoughts of Dallas, Connor went over the course in his head as he waited for the checkered flag to signal his start. He knew that this run would place him higher in the ranks if he could keep his mind on the race. If he came in with a good time today, he would have all kinds of time later to pursue some of his hunches on who their suspect was.

Giving a thumbs up to J.T., Connor took off. On the side-lines, J.T. smiled to himself. *I wonder what excitement today will hold?* he thought.

Connor kept the bike at full throttle. He wanted to make

sure he put miles of distance in between himself and Dallas. The little witch might try to run him off the course again. She couldn't be trusted as far as he was concerned – sheriff or no sheriff.

Flying over potholes and jutting granite, Connor's confidence soared. He had already passed several riders, leaving them in his dust. His eyes scanned everything – his gauges, the terrain, and the riders up front, but mostly his side mirrors. He was searching for the curvaceous and sinfully sexy rider in black.

The next rider got off to a good start, feeling confident that today *he* would overtake any and all riders...even Connor O'Reilly.

The terrain wasn't as demanding as day one's, but it still required concentration and skill to maneuver through Mother Nature's challenges. Pushing the limits of safety, he used his skill and nerve to increase his lead.

Trusting his instincts had kept him on top all these years, and because he trusted his instincts, he knew he had to watch his back. He knew he had made enemies during his years on the racing circuit, but racing motorcycles was not his first love. Illegal betting, scamming his fellow riders, and other disreputable deeds were what had kept him living the high life for the past ten years. It was a lifestyle he intended to continue.

Everything he knew, he had learned from his old man. Yah, his father had been a low-life, never amounting to anything. He had even done some time for his crimes. But his son, ever the astute student, had watched his father and studied where he had made his mistakes. He learned from them, refined his moves, and turned them into a bloody good living for himself.

Everything had been going great until South America. That scam hadn't worked out as he had planned. He thought he had worked out every last detail. He had left nothing to chance, or so he thought.

That was the one time he hadn't trusted his instincts. He realized now he should have cut his losses when the routine things started going wrong. He didn't believe in superstition, but he should have.

The lost luggage. The screwed-up hotel reservations. The damn P.I. who had popped up out of nowhere.

Then to top it off, he had ended up smack dab in the middle of a vicious bar fight. In his attempt to get away, he had crashed into a table of local gangsters engrossed in a high-stakes poker game. When they joined in the brawl, he had scooped the cash up from the table and hightailed it out a side door.

He got out relatively unscathed by leaving his friends and the P.I. behind. Not once did he feel any remorse about leaving them to the mercy of the man who obviously had held the winning hand. He just let the chips fall where they may – so to speak.

Guilt was an unfamiliar feeling to him, and when he thought he felt twinges of it, he reminded himself that he was fifty thousand dollars richer. That helped ease his conscience.

He had escaped that day by the skin of his teeth. Not trusting his instincts had definitely been a hard lesson. But he had learned. He *always* learned from his mistakes.

He turned his concentration back to overtaking the rider in front of him. He had planned on keeping an eye on Sheriff Nolan, but he hadn't seen her since he left the start line. He also wanted to find out more information about this O'Reilly dude.

Something about him and their relationship to one another didn't jive.

THE RIDER AT the back of the pack was barely holding his position but could care less. He had wanted to turn his life around, and racing motorcycles seemed to be his out. Once he had gotten a taste of the straight life, he couldn't seem to get enough of it. His past was littered with a variety of crime. An unwanted connection to the Hell's Angels and lots of jail time. His pals back home still couldn't believe he'd turned legit. They still tried to enlist his services for various unlawful adventures, but he always turned them down. He had done his time and wasn't interested in doing more.

One thing was for certain: He wasn't very good at being a criminal. He always seemed to get caught. He hated jail.

There was one advantage about living a hard life though: You always knew when something was creeping up your back. Something was happening at this race. He didn't know what it was, and he didn't really care, but he prayed it wouldn't involve him.

He was clean and planned on keeping it that way.

CHAPTER 11

WHEN DALLAS PULLED into the first checkpoint, she was disheartened to see that Connor was already there. Oh, she knew he was in front of her, but she had hoped that maybe he had fallen off a cliff or something.

No such luck.

This checkpoint was a service stop, so she took advantage of the fifteen minutes allotted to check over her bike and make some personal observations.

Alex Cross was also in ahead of her, and he was up to something. Dallas watched as he got ready to leave the start line.

He was scanning the streets. Not like a curious bystander, but like someone who knew just what to look for and where to find it. It was almost as if he were casing out each home and looking for weaknesses, cars in the driveway, and ease of access.

Yah, she thought, *this one really deserves some watching.* Dallas kept a careful eye on him until he left the checkpoint.

He was too smooth. Too confident. There was something about him that tweaked her cop radar. It frustrated her to no end that Betty's search was taking so long, but there was nothing more she could do at this point. Dallas waited her turn to be timed. She was holding her own from yesterday. She hadn't lost or gained, and that was good because it would allow her to be in with the leaders and give her the opportunity to keep an eye on Connor and Mr. Alex Cross.

She watched the riders who were getting their time cards checked. Morelli was one of them. She thought he seemed a little paranoid. Always looking over his shoulder.

He moved like an ex-con. He had that slouch that comes from not wanting to draw attention to himself, but in Morelli's case, it did quite the opposite. He had that quick shuffle, like someone who had spent some time in leg shackles. He never made direct eye contact, which was always a dead give-away for an ex-con. He looked worried and that bothered Dallas. She wondered what he was up to. Maybe he bore closer scrutiny than she first thought. The only problem was that the guy pulling off these heists was confident and Morelli was obviously the opposite.

Or a really good actor.

AT THE END of the day, the top riders remained the same. Nothing out of the ordinary had taken place, and all the riders had made good time.

Dallas decided to bug Betty one more time to find out if she had anything more for her. She headed off to her trailer and almost made it to the door when she heard Grams shout out to her.

"Yoo-hoo, Dallas. Come and see what I just bought."

Grams was decked out in her usual eccentric style, only this one was right over the top – a metallic purple tank dress, stopping about mid-thigh. Over top of it she wore her beat-up, red-leather riding jacket. Her pool cue legs were covered with fuchsia, knee-high leather boots.

Christ, Dallas thought, *she looks like a retired prostitute – a really old retired prostitute.*

Teetering on her three-inch purple heels, Grams asked, "What do you think, Dallas? I got an excellent deal for this get-up down at the thrift shop."

Dallas didn't know whether to laugh or cry, and she sure as hell didn't want to walk beside her. She loved Grams dearly, but at this particular moment, she didn't want to be caught dead next to her.

"Nice Grams."

Dallas truly didn't know what else to say.

"I knew you'd like it dear. It had 'me' written all over it."

Hustling Grams into the trailer before anyone could see her, Dallas said, "Let's start dinner."

"Oh, all right dear." Grams followed her inside the trailer.

"This is the outfit I'm wearing to the line-dancing tonight. I'll be taking someone's breath away."

"Yeah or making them blind," Dallas muttered to herself.

"Did you ride well today, Dallas?"

"Yeah Grams. I'm in with the leaders again. Did Betty call by any chance?" she asked

"No honey, but your laptop there says, 'You've got mail.'"

CHAPTER 12

CONNOR HAD J.T. drive the trailer to the final checkpoint for the day. It wasn't exactly the Waldorf, but at least they could bunk down for the night and attempt to cook their own meals if they were really desperate. It wasn't like his condo in Pueblo, but it would do. He had J.T. install a computer system with an uplink to the FBI's database. This would allow him to run a check on anyone he found suspicious. He now had several prospective suspects whose information he had programmed in, so he asked for profiles on each one.

Sometimes it took a good hour or so to download the information he wanted. So instead of waiting in the trailer, Connor decided to go and get a bite to eat. He wasn't desperate enough yet to cook his own meal. Leaving the computer processing the profiles, he left in search of the local pub.

When Connor arrived, he found Dallas happily seated at the table with J.T. and a couple of the other riders. Choosing not to make a scene, Connor sat himself at the opposite end of the table but in full view of Dallas. He had no idea what he was eating; his concentration was focused on trying to burn a hole through Dallas' forehead. He watched her back straighten when she became aware of his presence.

"So, O'Reilly, any problems with your plugs today?" Dallas asked sarcastically.

"Bitch," Connor snapped.

The rest of the meal was a battle of wills. Connor was the first to tire of the game. Making his excuses, he left the pub in a huff, taking what was left of his meal to go. The walk from the pub to the trailer did nothing to calm his disposition. How could someone who infuriated him so much, arouse him so completely?

Slamming the trailer door shut behind him, he kicked a beer can that had been left on the floor, realizing too late that it was still full. The can made a perfect arc as it flew through the air. Hitting the edge of the table, it sailed across the stained top, hit the wall, and spun on its side, spraying beer and foam over everything in the trailer, including him.

That caps it, he thought. *Damn stupid woman has me spinning my tires, and I had to make matters worse by kissing her the other night.* Calling himself every kind of fool as he rummaged under the cabinets for a cloth to clean up the mess, his mind drifted back to that kiss. He had never in his life been so fired up by a simple kiss.

Just thinking about it he felt a tightening in his stomach... and below. No matter how hard Connor tried, he just couldn't get Dallas out of his mind.

Yes, he was furious at the stupid practical joke that he thought she had played. Yes, he thought she was too damned sexy for her own good. Yes, he wanted to throttle her. So, he made up his mind that this was exactly what he was going to do.

Slamming the door behind him, he headed off in the

direction of Dallas' trailer. What he needed to say to her just couldn't wait. He was so determined to confront her that he didn't bother to check his computer.

That simple mistake would put him one step behind in the investigation.

The six-day race was so grueling that all anyone had time to do was eat and sleep. But Connor knew that he wouldn't be able to do the latter until he had it out with Dallas. Striding off to her trailer, jaw set, eyes glaring, Connor knew that nothing would stop him from shaking some sense into the stubborn redhead.

Nothing except the six-foot-five wall of solid muscle that he had just slammed in to.

"Whoa there, fella. You okay? the behemoth asked.

His hands engulfed Connor's shoulders as he pushed him away.

"Holy shit. Where'd you come from?"

Connor stared slacked-jawed at the size of the man in front of him. *His mama sure fed him a lot of spinach when he was a baby.*

Patrick chuckled. He was used to people's reaction to his size. He was extremely tall and had a mountain of strength that came with his height. Extending his ham-sized hand, he said, "Patrick Ryan. And you are?"

"O'Reilly. Connor O'Reilly."

"A fellow Irishman and apparently the one I'm supposed to beat in this race," Patrick said with a smirk.

"Yeah, if you can. Now if you'll excuse me, I'm in a hurry."

Dallas got up from her computer to answer the knock at

the door, but instantly regretted it when she saw who was standing on the other side.

Connor had every intention of giving her a very large piece of his mind, but when he saw her standing there in nothing but a long T-shirt that left nothing to the imagination, all his anger went out the window. Not giving her the chance to tell him to get out or go to hell, Connor walked her back into the tiny living space of her trailer and quietly closed the door. Anticipating another tirade, Dallas steeled herself for a fight.

Connor's face betrayed nothing about his mood and the first statement out of his mouth had her head spinning. "Has anyone ever told you how incredibly sexy you are?"

Dallas' jaw dropped, giving Connor the opportunity he needed to close the gap between them. Cupping her face in his hands and pulling her towards him, he slowly lowered his head until their lips met.

Softly at first, butterfly caresses.

When she didn't resist, Connor deepened the kiss. Their tongues met with a soft touch, which quickly turned hot and frantic.

Hearts pounding, the kiss took them both to a different level of enlightenment. Neither had experienced sexual arousal of this intensity before.

Connor couldn't keep his hands still. He needed to touch her, all of her: her face, shoulders, breasts. They were so mesmerized by each other that neither noticed that Connor had backed Dallas up against her bed. A little push was all it took to tumble the two of them into what was soon to be heaven.

Connor's mouth captured her pebbled nipple through the material of her T-shirt. This sent fiery blasts of desire to the core of her womanhood. Putting his hands under the material and pushing it up, he exposed her to his seeking mouth. Kissing first one breast then the other, he drove her to the brink of ecstasy.

Dallas couldn't wait to feel him naked against her. She ripped at his shirt, frustrated that it wasn't cooperating. So, she gave it a hard tug, pulling it open and sending buttons flying in all directions. Gaining access to his hard-muscled chest, she ran her hands skillfully over his nipples bringing forth a groan of pleasure. From whom neither knew. Both were entirely aroused.

Scraping her nails down his back, Dallas urged him closer, opening her legs to him, wanting to feel all of him covering her. His obvious arousal pressed against her stomach and his hips began moving in that age-old rhythm.

Dallas fought for control. Wanting to give more of herself, she wrapped her legs around his waist. Dallas rolled Connor onto his back, straddling him, not once breaking away from their erotic kiss.

She moved away from his mouth to trail moist kisses down his chest, licking his nipples, just as he had done to her. Her hands caressed his rock-hard abs and then ventured down to his navel. She paused over the button to his jeans, looking up only briefly to observe the barely suppressed desire radiating from his gorgeous blue eyes. Connor watched as she stripped him of the last barrier between them, releasing his straining arousal.

Dallas moved lower but was stopped when she felt Connor's hands urging her back up to his lips.

He was thrilled that she would want to take their first time to such a level of intimacy, but Connor knew that he wouldn't be able to last a minute once he felt her mouth on him.

Gazing at Connor's face, Dallas was empowered by the complete look of desire radiating from his eyes. She felt so incredibly dominant knowing that it was her that caused this reaction in him. She felt herself pulsing at the thought of him inside of her.

CONNOR HAD NEVER experienced anything as passionate and primal as what he was feeling at this moment. There was only him and Dallas and the lust that raged between them. Fighting for control, he moved over her and with her. Kisses, savage and intense, pushed him to the edge. Her nipples hardened under his ministrations. His hand dipped lower finding her hot, wet, and ready for him. He replaced his fingers with his mouth and brought her to the brink. Connor felt Dallas' orgasm. Once her breathing had returned to normal, he began kissing her again. Teasing little kisses meant to frustrate and arouse. When the passion began to build once more, he deepened the advance plundering her mouth and breasts.

"Now...please, Connor."

"Look at me, Dallas."

He wanted to see the passion in her eyes when he entered her. Watch her rise again with him to the peak.

Connor moved over Dallas and slowly penetrated her moist, hot core. He was sure that nothing in the world ever felt as good and as right as this moment with this woman in his arms.

Their climax was simultaneous and explosive. Each was a long time returning to normal.

The day's events and the sex left them exhausted. Just as they were about to drift off to sleep, the trailer door crashed open.

"Dallas, I'm back," Grams screeched from the doorway.

"Ohh, damn. I forgot about her," Dallas whispered to Connor.

"I'll be right out, Grams," she yelled back to her grandmother.

"Quick, put your clothes on."

Grams didn't bother to wait for Dallas to answer. She barged into the room and stood over Connor and Dallas smiling.

"Well, well, well, hello there! Nice hunk of meat, Dallas."

Dallas didn't think she had ever been so mortified.

"Hmm, I see you thought so too, honey. Look at all those teeth marks."

Connor just about died of embarrassment. Who the hell was this?

"I'm Dallas' grandma, sonny, and if you ever tire of her, I'll give you a run for your money."

That did it. Dallas groaned, her humiliation complete.

"Grams, please close the door so we can get dressed."

"Sure honey. But neither of you have anything that I haven't seen before."

"Grams!!"

Connor wrapped a blanket around his waist and walked to the little bathroom. He had deduced that "Grams" wasn't going anywhere when she made no move to leave. She looked like she wanted to stick around for the next show.

He didn't want to think about what had just happened, so he decided it was better just to make a quick exit.

DALLAS WAS SLOW to wake up the next morning, but when she did, the first thing she noticed was that her body was aching, and it had nothing to do with sitting on a bike for the last 150 miles. The second was the smell of coffee.

"He seems like a nice young man, honey," Grams commented when Dallas reached for the mug she was holding.

"Yah, I know."

"Nice butt too."

"Yah, I know Grams."

"Any good in bed?"

"Grams!"

"Boy, aren't you lucky that I decided to stay for the step-dance competition, otherwise we may have had an embarrassing situation on our hands."

Like that wasn't embarrassing enough? Dallas thought to herself.

It was probably better that Connor had left. She was sure he hadn't really showed up for some casual sex, and it was quite possible that whatever words they would have spoken to each other would have been the wrong ones.

Dallas knew that she'd have to talk to Connor sooner or later about the case and her suspicions around Alex Cross. He was her prime suspect in this cat burglary thing. Her background check on him came back with a few run-ins with the law but no convictions.

In fact, on paper Mr. Morelli looked like the guilty party. The problem was Morelli always got caught. The Heirloom Bandit was elusive to the point of almost being a phantom. Dallas couldn't see Morelli having that much finesse.

Yeah, she'd have to talk to Connor about this. Her gut was telling her that Cross was their man.

CHAPTER 13

DAY THREE DAWNED gray and damp. The miserable weather matched the mood of most of the riders as they prepared themselves and their bikes for the third leg of the race.

He was on the sidelines waiting his turn. He watched as the first racers left the start line. The headlines in the morning news claimed the Heirloom Bandit had struck again, and the local police were at a loss as to who the thief could be. The article mentioned that the townspeople were up in arms about their quiet little community being violated by this culprit and wanted the FBI involved. Fat chance, he thought. They had better things to do with their time than track down a petty thief. He finished looking over his bike and headed off to the start line. He decided not to give this nonsense with the FBI another thought. Today would be a good day.

O'Reilly had already left and the pretty, little local sheriff was up after him. What struck him as odd was they didn't look like a couple that had enjoyed a romp in the hay the previous night. There was no passion-filled kiss for luck – not even a peck on the cheek. Maybe O'Reilly hadn't gotten lucky after all. Maybe his instincts were off...again. A brief thought that he was losing his touch floated through his mind. He knew he'd have to keep his wits about him.

Oh well, whatever had happened, he was grateful for last night's gift. It was just by chance, he'd spotted O'Reilly entering Dallas' trailer. A craving for a cigarette and some fresh air had put him at the right place at the right time. Knowing that they were both accounted for, at least for the time being, he decided to put his plan into action a bit sooner than he had intended.

He was confident that O'Reilly would never do anything in retaliation for Dallas' alleged prank. He was too macho and had too much integrity to pay back a woman. But that didn't mean he couldn't.

His plan would kill, figuratively speaking of course, two birds with one stone. The bitch cop would probably be injured – maybe even seriously. That would get her out of his hair.

Whatever, it would be enough to end her chances of getting too close to the truth. When the story came out about them tampering with each other's bike, O'Reilly would be disqualified for causing injury to another rider. Then he, being the best racer on the circuit, would go on to the winner's circle and claim his prize, and no one would be the wiser.

Oh, he'd show just the right amount of disappointment and regret for his wayward fellow competitors in his acceptance speech, but in reality, he wouldn't feel the least bit of remorse. He couldn't put his finger on why, but he was beginning to hate and distrust O'Reilly.

Last night, he had waited to make sure Connor wasn't coming out of Dallas' trailer anytime soon before heading to the impound area. He'd thought up his little plan the day before. Better to eliminate some competition early on than have something unforeseen happen later. He'd almost ditched his idea when he started having the feeling that someone was following him. Nothing positive, just that "hairs on the back of your neck" feeling.

On the off chance that he was right, he would get someone else to execute his plan. He already knew where Dallas' bike was parked, so it was just a matter of feeding the information to his accomplice.

It was a shame that she had to get hurt – she was a beautiful woman.

CHAPTER 14

DALLAS WATCHED CONNOR leave the start line. The gray, misty dawn matched her mood. Was she second-guessing herself? She wondered why Connor had left without a word. Last night had been the most incredible experience she had ever had. Even this morning her body still tingled with desire. Maybe, she had just been a distraction to him. An itch to be scratched.

Maybe, she should just use this as a learning experience: Never mix pleasure with business.

Connor barely even looked at her when she pulled up beside him before the start of the race. A barely perceptible nod of his head was his only acknowledgement that she was even there. Hope that there would ever be a repeat performance died with his cold disregard in the light of day.

Well, if that was the way he was going to play it, she could play by those rules too.

Dallas was called to go off. She felt like she had lost some of her enthusiasm for the race; only the reminder that she was also working on a case got her started. Slinging mud, her tires skidded and then dug into the muck as she left the start line.

The first quarter mile or so of the course had been chewed up pretty badly by the previous riders. Everyone was bound and determined that today would be their best run, rotten conditions notwithstanding. Taking her time, she kept to a moderate speed until she was out of the worst of the ruts and mud. She knew that the first twenty or so miles of today's course were an old logging road that ran between the towns of Montrose and Gunnison.

A mile outside of Gunnison they would be on the Interstate for fifty-three miles. Even with the drizzle, this was the easiest start they had encountered yet.

It was the last sixty miles that would test her skill. It was all uphill, through heavily wooded timberland and old county roads. The route would take them through the dirt tracks to the next short section of the Interstate and then on back roads to the finish. The terrain was very rocky and crisscrossed with old creek beds. These conditions would be ripe for unexpected damage to the rider's motorcycle from all manner of hidden obstacles.

Someone had the foresight to mention on the route maps that riders should be careful of the drop-offs that ran along some of the granite outcroppings in this particular area. With that in mind, Dallas focused on keeping up an even pace without jeopardizing her safety.

At the end of the first Interstate section was a checkpoint. This was a time check only. The first fuel and repair check would be at the halfway point of the second leg. Dallas was glad she had kept a moderate speed to this point. It had helped her conserve gas and tires.

Entering the area, she noticed there were only a handful of riders waiting to have their cards validated, and Connor was not among them. He must have made good time. She wondered how far ahead he was.

Pulling to a stop by the timekeeper, Dallas unzipped her jacket pocket and removed her time card.

"You're making pretty good time, Nolan. Keep it up and you'll be in the top racers again."

The man put her time down and signed her card.

"How far ahead are the leaders?" Dallas asked, not really caring just making conversation.

"Not far, maybe ten, fifteen minutes. But be careful if you're thinking of making up time. From here to the Interstate it's pretty treacherous going, especially in these conditions."

"Thanks, I will."

Dallas pulled up to the line to wait for the signal to go. A chill ran down her spine. Pulling the collar on her jacket up higher in the back, she shivered.

"Boy, I hate cold, rainy days," she mumbled as she took off down the slight incline to the next section of the course.

The guy at the checkpoint was right, there were more twists and turns on this section than in an Agatha Christie novel. The motorcycle bounced over half-buried rocks and slid into the ruts left by the riders ahead.

Dallas had no choice but to hold back on her speed. She didn't want to – you don't make up time by going slower – but she knew that everyone else, unless they had a death wish, would have to do the same. This made her feel better about not making any progress at gaining on the leaders.

Getting herself into a routine of judging how much to accelerate on an incline and decelerate on the decline, she felt herself relax for the first time that day. The scenery was beautiful, even in the rain. Majestic pine and spruce, probably hundreds of years old, grew so thick in spots you couldn't see more than five or six feet into the forest. Dallas wondered how they had escaped the axe and chainsaw of the lumber companies. Trees like these would have been prime targets for the lumber business. Whatever the reason for the oversight, she was glad they still survived.

Dallas felt like a pioneer seeing the virgin countryside as it might have been in the 1800s. Untouched by the influx of settlers and entrepreneurs ready to make their fortunes at the expense of nature, it was as God had intended.

Coming to the crest of a hill, she had to stop her bike. The vista in front of her took her breath away: miles and miles of verdant, rolling forest and a light mist hanging above the tree line. Towering granite cliffs, some hundreds of feet high, interrupted the flow of green, and below her was a lake whose surface was disturbed only by the falling rain.

Dallas was awestruck. This adventure, this challenge, was changing her; would change her in more ways than she knew. Knowing she was wasting precious time, but reluctant to leave, she put the bike in gear and started down the ridge, picking up speed as she went. The track dipped sharply about halfway down where it cut through a narrow space between two house-sized boulders. Taking her focus off the terrain, she fixed her attention on maneuvering between the obstacles.

Too late, she realized that what she had thought was the continuation of the trail was actually a drop off to a rock-strewn creek bed twenty feet below. Braking as hard as she dared, Dallas turned the handlebars hard to the left.

The distance to the edge was rapidly closing.

CHAPTER 15

CONNOR PULLED INTO the second checkpoint well ahead of the pack. He had been beating himself up for the last two hours over his treatment of Dallas at the start of the day, but his mind had been on the reports that he had pulled off the computer when he got back to his trailer the night before. His suspicions regarding the individuals he inquired about had borne fruit, but it was the report on one Frank Morelli that had him intrigued.

This man seemed to have gotten into an awful lot of trouble over the course of his life. What was most interesting was that a lot of that trouble had occurred in places that coincided with hits by their suspect, not necessarily in the same time frame, but Connor was willing to overlook that...for the moment.

He knew he would have to share his findings with Dallas; after all, she was his contact with the local law enforcement. He was sure they could keep this on a strictly professional basis from now on, but if he was being honest with himself, he had to admit that their experience the previous night had been nothing short of amazing.

Connor had never expected to feel this way. Sure, he'd had sex with other partners, but it was just that. It was only sex – a satisfying biological function. No residual feelings. No desire to repeat the action, just a release.

With Dallas, it had been more than that. It had been like his first time – all feelings and sensations, his body alive for the touch of her. The feel of her softness surrounding him, bringing him to a fevered climax. Both of them tumbling over the edge together, each sighing the other's name at the moment of pure ecstasy. Then lying together wrapped in each other's arms as the passion built for yet another ride…that was, until her grandmother had walked in.

When he woke this morning, he still wanted her. He was having feelings for her that went beyond a one-night stand, and *that* scared the hell out of him. He had left her the night before without a word, and worst of all, he had all but ignored her this morning.

Connor decided to wait as long as he could at the time check. If she came in before he had to go off, he'd apologize, ask her out for dinner, and make it up to her.

"Hey Con, you okay? You look troubled. There's nothing wrong with the bike, is there?" J.T. said handing Connor a water bottle.

"Uh, no, the bike's okay. I was just wondering…never mind, it's not important."

"Whoa, wait a minute. You can't stand there looking like the world's about to end and tell me nothing's wrong. This is me…J.T. I know you, remember? Something's buggin' you. I can tell. Wouldn't have something to do with the case you're working on…*or*, maybe a beautiful redhead we both know, would it?"

J.T. was smug in his assessment of the situation.

Connor watched as rider after rider pulled into the check-point. There was Alex and Patrick Ryan, Franco and Balducci, and a few others whose names he didn't remember, but no Dallas. Worried, he walked over to Patrick.

"Hey Ryan, you didn't happen to see or pass Dallas Nolan, did you?"

"No, why?"

"No reason. I just thought she'd be in this group of riders."

"Do you think she's got trouble?"

The disappearance of the suspect Ryan was tracking last night suddenly took on ominous proportions. He'd been following his man for a while now, and just when it looked like he was getting close to catching him, the guy had vanished.

He was as slippery as an eel. Seemed to have a sixth sense, like he had eyes in the back of his head. Patrick hadn't able to pick him up after that, so he had just called it a night.

"Nah, she's probably just taking it easy today because of the weather and all." Connor was trying to reassure himself.

J.T. put his arm on Connor's shoulder.

"She's one of the best motorcycle riders I've seen – male or female. Dallas can take care of herself. You're probably right; she's just taking it easy. She'll be in any minute now."

But the look on J.T.'s face betrayed his growing concern.

"You're up, Con. I'll let her know you were worried about her. I'm sure she'll be appreciative."

"Bite me," Connor growled.

"I'll leave that delight up to the lady," J.T. laughed.

After Connor had left, J.T. hung back and waited for Dallas.

CHAPTER 16

SOMETHING WAS WRONG. That fact registered immediately in Dallas' brain. What that something was took her another second to comprehend. Her handlebars were turned all the way to the left. She should be turning in that direction – but she wasn't. She was still heading right for the cliff.

She straightened her handlebars and tried again. Hands and handlebars again turned to the left, yet she was still heading straight.

Time slowed. Everything around her blurred – every-thing, except the impending disaster in front of her. Understanding dawned.

Something, or someone, had loosened the retaining ring around the front wheel assembly. She could turn the handle-bars freely, but the wheel stayed straight. Dallas was headed straight for the drop-off, and there was nothing she could do about it. Thoughts of being smashed against the rocks at the bottom of the drop flashed through her mind.

How long would it take for someone to find her?

Would Connor be upset? Would he miss her?

Do something! her brain screamed.

Should she save herself? Save the motorcycle? Save both?

In the time it took for all this to pass through her mind, Dallas decided her course of action.

She had no choice but to drop the bike. If she did it right and turned the rear tire toward the drop maybe, just maybe, it would give her enough time to come to a stop before both of them went over. If not, she might have enough time to let go of the motorcycle and save herself.

Laying a bike down is a feat that requires guts and luck, especially with speed. Gritting her teeth, Dallas put the bike into a sideways slide and then leaned towards the ground. Because of the wet ground, the bike slid onto its side with no problem. The problem was that the momentum did not decrease – at first. Dallas felt the rocks cut into her leg as the weight of the bike rested on top of her. Her head hit a rock jutting out of the ground. Even with her helmet on there was enough force to make her see stars.

Her vision blurred. Please God, I can't black out. I have to know when to let go. I have to know when to let go...the mantra kept pounding in her head.

Slowly, her skid lost momentum. Would it be enough?

The rear wheel slid off the edge.

She could hear dislodged rocks and dirt bouncing off the cliff face. Dallas closed her eyes and held her breath.

Finally, she stopped. Her hands were locked in a death grip on the handgrips; her arm muscles burned with the effort it had taken to stay with the motorcycle. Sweat trickled down her face. Her breathing came in ragged gasps.

Afraid to move she slowly opened her eyes. The motorcycle had come to a stop with the rear wheel dangling over the drop. If she let go, it would go over, and quite possibly, so would she.

Think Dallas. Think. Arms shaking with fatigue Dallas willed her mind to function. *Pull the bike toward you.*

I can't. I don't have the strength.

You have to.

Brain and body warred with each other.

Come on, Dallas, you can do this.

Gritting her teeth, she willed her arms to work.

Adrenalin surged through her. Summoning what little strength she had left, she dug her boot heels into the mud to find purchase. Hooking first her right arm and then her left under the handlebars and heaving with all her might, Dallas managed to slowly pull the heavy motorcycle and herself away from the edge of the embankment.

She lay there spent; all thought of moving was foreign. Her only comfort was the cold chunk of metal resting on her legs.

Slowly her senses flickered to life, and she felt exhaustion, relief, and then pain.

Get up. You have to move.

I can't.

Yes, you can. You're wasting time.

Dallas slowly lifted the motorcycle up off her leg. A lightning bolt of pain shot to her knee. Please don't let it be broken.

Rolling to a sitting position, she felt from her ankle to her knee. She was pretty sure there was no fracture. It was probably a sprain. She pulled herself up and put all her weight on her uninjured leg, reluctant to stand on both. Dallas knew she had to get back on the motorcycle. She had already taken too much time getting herself up and was falling farther and farther behind in her time.

Gritting her teeth against the pain, Dallas forced her

injured leg to move. Lifting the motorcycle up, engaging the kickstand, Dallas hand tightened the retaining ring, hoping it would be enough to get her to the checkpoint.

She thanked her lucky stars that the kick-start was under her uninjured leg. She put her weight on the wounded ankle, moaning against the pain and pushed down on the kick-start.

Thank you, thank you, thank you.

The bike started on the first try. Dallas took off.

CONNOR PACED AT the finish line. He had already been waiting for over fifteen minutes and still she hadn't shown up. He was getting worried, and he really needed to apologize to Dallas for his behavior that morning.

The rain that had been falling at the start of the day had turned into a light mist, but the temperature had dropped about ten degrees. The cold was beginning to seep through the leather of Connor's jacket. The sounds of the over-revved engines of the motorcycles heading to impound were starting to grate on his nerves. Over the loud speaker he heard the name of the latest rider in, and it wasn't Dallas.

Where the hell is she?

Connor couldn't wait any longer. He had to get his bike to the impound. The rules were clear. If you were finished for the day, the bike went into impound; no exceptions. These rules allowed little room to tamper with the bikes. Cheating had been a problem in the past with riders trying to soup up their rides before the next leg, and this was the only way to put a stop it.

J.T. stayed behind after Connor left hoping that Dallas would show up in the next round of riders.

No such luck.

Checking his watch for the umpteenth time, J.T. was shocked to find that almost thirty minutes had passed since Connor had left. This was too long. Dallas only had fifteen minutes left before she would be disqualified. She should have been no more than ten minutes behind Connor even in the worst-case scenario. Apprehension crept up his spine. Pacing, he kept checking down the road and then his watch.

Still nothing. Every second that passed seemed like an hour.

"Where are you Dallas?"

The last of the day's riders had just passed through the checkpoint and still there was no sign of her. If she didn't come in soon, she'd be over her hour mark.

J.T. was ready to go looking when the sound of a solitary motorcycle could be heard in the distance.

Please, let that be Dallas.

J.T. hadn't realized that he had been holding his breath until it whooshed out of his lungs when he saw Dallas round the final bend into the checkpoint area.

She looked a wreck.

J.T. had to check his urge to run over to her. He stood his ground, knowing that any assistance before she crossed the finish line would disqualify her. The wait was agonizing.

When her bike finally passed the clocking area, he made his way over to her. Dallas saw J.T. standing on the sidelines – actually, two J.T.s. Shaking off the momentary vertigo, she rode over to check her time card.

Once she was through with her time check, J.T. rushed over to her. "What the hell happened to you, Dallas? Where have you been?"

There was concern in his voice, and it was mirrored in his eyes.

"Oh, I just thought I'd see how much fun it would be to try going over a cliff."

"What do you mean, going over a cliff? What the hell are you talking about, Dallas?"

"I think someone tried to kill me."

"What the…what do you mean someone tried to kill you? What happened?"

J.T. was becoming very anxious. Dallas wasn't making any sense. She was pale as death, and her body seemed to sway like a leaf in a breeze.

"Someone tried to kill me, that's what." She was getting angrier by the minute at the thought.

"Someone tried, but I was too smart for them. I ditched my bike to keep from going off a twenty-foot drop."

Dallas was shouting, her stomach was doing back flips, and she could taste bile in the back of her throat. She held her pounding head in her hands, willing herself not to throw up on his shoes. She was wasting time standing here arguing with J.T.

"Whoa up, Dallas. Let's get Connor; he'll know what to do."

He was concerned about why she was holding her head.

"Did you hit your head? Do you think you might have a concussion?"

J.T. wanted to make sure that she was okay and wouldn't fall flat on her face, but they needed to get Connor involved in this as well.

He was sure she wasn't exaggerating about what had happened, and because of that, they needed to get Connor and run through their list of suspects again. His profiling hadn't come up with any of them being violent, and that meant J.T. needed to do some more research as well.

But more importantly, they needed to get Dallas medical attention.

"I don't need Connor. I know what happened, and I know there's nothing I can do about it now. Someone backed off the retaining ring on my front wheel assembly. Someone who thinks I'm getting a little too close to solving this case."

Turning too quickly, Dallas almost lost her balance. She grabbed her head with one hand, and J.T. with the other while she waited for the world to stop spinning.

"Dallas, what's wrong?" J.T. asked, concern furrowing his brow.

"You hit your head when you dumped the bike didn't you?"

"It's nothing…just a little dizzy, that's all." Dallas closed her eyes and willed the world to stop spinning,

"I think it's more than dizzy. I think you might have a concussion. You can't run a race tomorrow with your head swimming. I'm telling the timer that you're backing out of the race."

"You will like hell. You're not my family."

Dallas threw her leg over the bike and revved the engine.

"I'm not going to quit because of a little bump on the head and let Connor get all the credit for catching the Heirloom Bandit. Besides, I'm sure that I'm one step away from nailing this S.O.B."

J.T. grabbed her leg to hold her back. Hissing in pain, Dallas slapped his hand away. J.T. didn't miss the look of pain that crossed her face. Now he was really getting concerned.

"What's wrong with your leg?"

On closer inspection, he noticed her leathers were torn and her leg was bleeding.

"Dallas you're hurt. You can't go on like this; you need to see a doctor."

She glared at him her anger finally boiling over. "Don't lecture me! Just get away from me and leave me alone. I've already lost enough time, J.T. I'll never make it up now. Just get the hell out of my way and leave me alone – please."

With her last words, her voice was barely a whisper. She turned her head just in time to throw up, barely missing J.T.'s toes.

J.T. grabbed her shoulders and held her steady while she emptied the contents of her stomach.

"You're hurt. I can't let you ride in this condition; I'd never be able to forgive myself if something happened to you. Listen to me, Dallas. Connor needs to be told about this. You two are supposed to be working together on this thing. You're probably right; you're getting too close. You two need to put your heads together and figure out who it is."

Dallas turned away from J.T., closing her eyes when her stomach threatened to empty again.

"Screw you. We're not going to do this right now. I need to get my bike to impound before they disqualify me. It'll take more than a bump on the head to stop me from catching this jerk. NOW, GET OUT OF MY WAY!"

She knew her shot at apprehending her suspect hinged on staying in this race. She knew she sounded desperate, but she really wasn't. It was just frustration. She was sure that her suspect knew she was getting too close. Giving her bike full throttle, Dallas took off, leaving behind a rooster tail of mud and a very concerned, very confused J.T.

He had to find Connor – and quick.

Connor was waiting at the trailer for J.T.

"Where the hell was she?" He had been just a little concerned. He knew he had run an excellent time, but that didn't account for Dallas being this late. His worry grew when he saw the look on his friend's face when he walked up to the trailer.

"What's wrong, J.T.?" Connor tried to sound calm. "Did you see Dallas? Did she finish?"

"Something weird is going on Con, and I don't like it, not one little bit. You were with her last night, weren't you?"

"Yeah, so what?" Connor replied guardedly.

"So, somebody tampered with her bike. I mean seriously tampered with her bike. When she finally came into the checkpoint she was shaken and pale. She's hurt and really, really angry."

"She's hurt! How bad?" Connor grabbed J.T. by the arms.

"Bad enough that I don't think she should finish the race. Her leather pants were torn, she had a gash on her leg, and I'm pretty sure she might have a concussion."

Connor's stomach dropped to his knees. "She has a concussion! She could kill herself if she tries to ride with a concussion!"

J.T. ignored Connor's tirade. He knew it was just his concern for Dallas talking.

"She's pretty sure it was her suspect. I think you two should do some serious talking about where you're going with this investigation before someone gets killed."

"I'm going to sit down with the information we've retrieved

so far and re-evaluate my thoughts on the profile. If this guy is getting desperate enough to resort to attempted murder, then we need to take a deeper look at our suspects." J.T. pulled out a chair and sat down at the computer.

"I agree that all three of us need to sit down and compare notes, but first, we need to get Dallas medical attention," Connor said.

"I suggested she get medical attention, but she's having no part of that," J.T. informed Connor.

"Well, that's her problem," Connor replied. "We'll get her there if we have to drag her kicking and screaming."

Connor's mind raced. He had his idea about who could be irresponsible enough to do something like this. What he needed was proof. His emotions were in an uproar.

He didn't want Dallas angry with him, but that was too bad. They had to look after first things first and getting her to a doctor was top on the agenda.

"I need to talk to her. Where is she?"

"She went to her trailer after she took her bike to impound, Con. She probably thinks she can look after her injuries with a Band-Aid and an aspirin. I seriously think the girl wants to make this collar. You know, prove that she's as good as the FBI."

J.T. wasn't being malicious; his profiler instincts told him that Dallas just wanted to prove herself.

"I don't give a damn who gets credit for the arrest, J.T., but this guy is changing his MO. He's never done or tried to do physical harm to anyone before. What's happened to change him from robbery to attempted homicide?"

The concern in Connor's voice revealed the depth of his feelings for Dallas to J.T.

Looking over Connor's shoulder, J.T. said, "Speak of the devil. Dallas is at the door, and she's loaded down with files. Looks like she was having the same thoughts we are about sharing information. But if it's all the same to you, I think we need to get her medical attention first. Better let her in before she passes out."

Dallas stood teetering on the doorstep, laden down with all her files. She hadn't even bothered to change out of her riding clothes. She was still wearing the torn, bloodstained leathers. She looked and felt like hell. Her attempt to wipe the dirt from her face had only moved the dirt around.

J.T. couldn't hide his concern at her appearance. Connor's face said the same when he saw the condition she was in.

J.T. turned to Conner, "If it's all the same to you, Con, I think we should get her to a doctor right now; any brain storming can wait."

Dallas didn't have a chance to knock. Connor pulled the door open just as she was getting ready to kick it with her foot. She was really pissed, and she wanted to take her anger out on something. After she dumped her files on the table, she ranted on for a full minute about how she felt.

"…and to top it all off, I could have been *killed* going over that cliff. Someone wants me out of this race – or dead."

She would have gone on, but the violence of her tirade had her head swimming again and before she could settle down, she threw up – all over Connor's shoes. Connor grabbed her before she slid to the floor. Ignoring the mess on his runners, he bellowed, "Cliff. What cliff? What are you talking about?"

Connor shot J.T. a quelling look. "You didn't say anything about a cliff!"

Dallas punched Connor in the arm to get his attention. "Excuse me, but I think I'm going to throw up again."

Dallas felt a wave of nausea wash over her. Her face paled, her head swam, and she had a sudden loss of balance.

Putting his hands on her shoulders to steady her and not thinking, he gave her a quick shake. "You're going to the hospital *right now!*"

"Don't do that."

Dallas thought for sure she would throw up all over Connor's runners again. Swallowing, she managed to get her stomach back where it belonged.

"Get your hands off me. I don't need any help."

Reality finally sunk in for Connor. It finally dawned on him that whoever had done this really had wanted Dallas dead, and it was only her quick thinking that had saved her.

His first impulse was to question her, but he could tell by the gray pallor of her skin that pursuing that train of thought would have to wait.

"You need to see a doctor, Dallas. You could have a concussion."

"I *don't have* a concussion!"

Her voice shook with rage, and the tenuous reign she had on her emotions finally snapped. Fury drove her, and all rational thought vanished. Dallas was about let go with another right hook when another wave of nausea overtook her. The force of her swing drove her around in a circle; her fist just missing Connor's face. Staggering, she lost her balance and toppled towards him. Her vision blurred, and she crumpled in a heap on the ground.

"That's it! You're going to the hospital. NOW!"

Connor scooped her up in his arms. "Damn wildcat is going to land one of those punches one of these days."

Dallas didn't have the strength to argue with him anymore, so she gave into the comforting feel of his arms and closed her eyes.

The ashen color of her skin scared him. Connor's heart twisted in his chest. Trying to remain calm he said, "We'll find out who did this, Dallas, and we'll do it together."

CHAPTER 17

DALLAS WAS PUTTING up quite a fuss. She glared at the three men who were hovering over her. The doctor was fast losing his patience, and Connor and J.T. weren't helping him any with their flip comments.

"I'm *not* staying in the hospital. All I need is rest. Sleep. That's all."

The doctor looked at her with frustration. "You have a nasty gash on your leg and possibly a mild concussion, but you still need someone to wake you up every couple of hours to make sure you don't slip in to a coma, young lady."

He was being melodramatic and his patronizing tone was starting to irritate her.

Giving up trying to talk any sense into Dallas, the doctor turned his attention to Connor and J.T.

"Can one of you help me out here?"

"Hey, we tried. She's got a mind of her own, Doc," Connor replied.

Exasperated, the doctor threw up his hands. "I am *not* releasing you from this hospital unless someone takes responsibility for you. If one of these two *gentlemen* is willing to do that, then you can go. Otherwise, you're stuck here for the next twenty-four hours. The choice is yours."

"Doc, can I see you for a minute alone?" Connor said without hesitation. He took the doctor aside.

"J.T. and I'll make sure she sees reason and does what she's told."

"Don't you start patronizing me too. I'll do what I want," Dallas ranted.

"No Dallas, you'll do what *I want*," Connor threatened.

"Over my dead body," she replied.

"*That* can be arranged you know." Connor shot her a scathing look.

"Oh yah. More threats? Maybe you should just shoot me and get it over with."

Her head felt like it was in a vise. The doctor said it was a combination of emotional stress from the accident and a so-called mild concussion.

Boy, she can be irritating when she wants to, Connor thought.

"I'll chalk that remark up to childishness and fatigue, okay little girl?"

The doctor looked back and forth between his patient and Connor. He wondered what was going on between them, but knew better than to ask. Shaking his head, he walked out and gave them the privacy they obviously needed. J.T. was close on the doctor's heels.

"Do you honestly want to be here alone?" asked Connor. "Whoever did this is out there and could possibly come back here or to your trailer. Don't be a hero, Dallas. Just let J.T. and I help. If you don't want to be alone with me, then I'll just make sure J.T. never leaves the trailer."

Dallas sighed. The cop in her knew he was right: It was better to be safe with Connor than sorry alone.

She nodded her head.

"I don't want Grams to know what happened or she'll make me leave the race. So if you promise me you will keep this quiet, I'll go with you. If nothing else, it'll give us a chance to discuss our prospective suspects." Connor and Dallas walked out of the hospital room together. J.T. was waiting with the doctor out in the hall.

"She's decided to come with us, Doc," Connor stated the obvious.

"Wake her every couple of hours," he said.

"Ask her a couple of simple questions just to make sure she's coherent. If she forgets something simple like her name, bring her back to the ER right away."

"You've got it, Doc."

"About the knee. A few stitches and a sprain. I cleaned out the wound and sutured and bandaged it. She'll need to ice it. The pain killers I gave you should help the knee and her head. Give her one or two every four hours. Other than that, she'll be fit as a fiddle in a couple of days."

Connor bent to pick Dallas up.

"Get your hands off of me, you moron. I can walk."

"Shut up woman. Just shut the hell up."

Booking no further argument, Connor carried Dallas to his truck. They drove back to her trailer in silence. She didn't have to worry about dealing with her ditzy grandmother. Grams had left a note pinned to the door of the trailer letting Dallas know she had a "hot date" and probably wouldn't be back that night "if she got lucky". Dallas grabbed some clean clothes and left.

Connor was relieved. It would be easier to watch her at his place. Settling her into the bed, he gave her two of the painkillers the doctor had prescribed, and then he tucked the covers in around her. He sat down on the edge of the bed reluctant to leave her. He kept thinking how close he had come to losing her and wondering why the hell that mattered so much.

Dallas' eyes slowly closed as fatigue finally claimed her. Connor pushed a lock of hair away from her forehead, leaned over, and kissed her lightly on the lips.

"I'm sorry, Dallas. I promise I'll find who did this."

He stayed with her until he heard her deep, even breathing. She had finally fallen asleep. Connor watched her for a few more minutes. This woman was getting under his skin, and it scared the hell out of him. It couldn't be love – could it? He'd promised himself that it would never happen again. Katherine had made sure of that.

But then, he'd never felt for Katherine what he was feeling for Dallas, not in all the years they were together.

J.T. found Connor with Dallas when he came into the trailer. "How's she doing?" he whispered.

Connor rolled his head from side-to-side, trying to ease the tension that had him in knots. "She's finally asleep. I think I'll stay with her for awhile."

"Connor you can't stay up all night. You've got to race in the morning."

"I know. Maybe we can take shifts."

"Sure, man. No problem. You get something to eat. You haven't had anything since this morning, and then get some rest. I'll wake her in a couple of hours, and then you can take the second shift."

With one final look at Dallas' sleeping form, Connor walked into the living area to his laptop. He double-checked all the profiles of his possible suspects.

Something just didn't feel right. Why had the thief changed his tactics? There had never been any violence during his break-ins – not even when he was almost unmasked by the old man during the robbery in Texas. Could it be that he had planned something really big this time, and they were too close to discovering who he was? He knew he should get something to eat, but he was too upset.

One question kept replaying in his mind: Who stood to gain from taking Dallas out of the picture? And why Dallas? She was just a small-town sheriff? Could it be that their unsub didn't know he was FBI?' Mulling that fact over, he decided maybe that could work to his advantage. Connor poured over his printouts for an hour, looking for something to jump out at him. But in the end, only one rider came to mind: Frank Morelli. But still, there was still something about his theory that just didn't fit.

When Dallas was up to it, he'd get her input on possible perps.

WELL, I GUESS the sheriff is no longer a threat. She wasn't dead, but she wouldn't be sticking her nose where it didn't belong either. Even if she was well enough to continue, she was far enough back in the standings that she wouldn't be in his way. Not in the race and especially not in his extracurricular activities.

His only other competition in the race now was Connor

O'Reilly, who he now knew was an FBI agent probably assigned to his case. He'd had a feeling that there was more to the man than he first thought, so he did some digging and discovered his identity. He wasn't worried though. He knew he could come up with an effective way of eliminating him as well.

CHAPTER 18

ALEX HAD HEARD the other racers talking about what had happened to Dallas. Wanting to portray the ever-concerned friend, he headed over to O'Reilly's trailer to check in on her. He wanted to see for himself how bad off she was. Reaching the trailer door, he gave it two quick taps.

J.T. answered.

Nodding his head in greeting, Alex said, "Just heard about what happened. Thought I'd drop by and see how the patient was doing."

"Her head and leg are a little sore, but she's a trooper. Come on in."

"I don't want to intrude."

"The more the merrier," J.T. said sarcastically, gesturing for him to come in.

O'Reilly and Frank Morelli were already standing around the bed.

What the hell was Frank doing here? Alex wondered. It made him uneasy to be in such close quarters with these three men, but he kept his cool.

"How are you feeling, Dallas? Head traumas can be nasty business."

"I'll be fine. J.T. and Connor are watching over me like two little mother hens. Neither one of them can cook worth a damn, but I appreciate the attempt.

"I don't know if you know Frank..." she said by way of introduction.

Alex gave a brief nod to his nemesis. "Yeah, we've met."

Morelli didn't say anything. He just stood there looking smug with an "I got here before you did" look on his face.

"I just came over to let you know that I'm offering my assistance to O'Reilly in his endeavor to find the culprit who did this. Puts a bad name on the NSDE and races in general, really."

Fancy words from my prime suspect, Dallas thought.

"That's very kind of you Alex," she said sweetly. "I'm sure Connor appreciates your offer."

"No problem. We have to stick together. We certainly can't let some malfeasant taint the race."

J.T. couldn't shake the feeling that this guy wasn't what he seemed. He was too nice, too caring, and way too arrogant. All of his internal warning bells rang. His profiler instincts were screaming. This guy was up to something, and J.T. had the feeling that it wasn't good.

Dallas was trying to remain cordial toward the unexpected visitors, but it was becoming more and more difficult to be in such close quarters with them.

J.T. mistook the strained look around her eyes as pain. "Do you need another pain killer, Dallas?"

"Yeah, maybe one." She used this as her excuse to bid the two men good night.

"Sorry gentlemen, seems I'm not as up to having company

as I thought. Besides, I have to be well rested for the race tomorrow."

She watched to see what effect her statement would have on Cross and Morelli.

"Quite understandable. Feel better, Dallas." Cross kept his smile in place. He leaned over and brushed an innocent, seemingly brotherly kiss, across her forehead. Morelli smiled and offered a "get well" wish, and then they both left.

Dallas could barely contain her shudder of disgust. *Creep*. She just knew that Cross was her man.

HE BARELY MANAGED *to hide the wicked grin that played around the corners of his mouth. They were all idiots. He walked among them, stealing from them, hurting them, almost killing them, and they were oblivious to it all. The thrill of it was like a sexual high, and he rode it for all it was worth.*

His goal was to win – any and every way possible.

CHAPTER 19

PATRICK RYAN WATCHED Connor's trailer. He had seen his man heading in that direction. He had also heard about Dallas' accident and just knew his guy had something to do with it.

Patrick had heard some complaints from the other riders about missing money and jewelry and knew he was behind that as well.

The guy must be the biggest egotist in the world...or the stupidest. Well, Patrick thought, *your time is about to run out smart guy. You're going down.*

Patrick could tell that his suspect was getting desperate. There were too many people trying to stop him. He also knew the man was feeling confident that any threat from Dallas and her small-town police force had been was taken care of.

He knew his perp's next move would be on O'Reilly. He had heard some of the other racers talking about him being FBI. Made sense that they would have an agent involved. Now that the cat was out of the bag, O'Reilly had better watch his back.

Following his suspect, Patrick ducked into the doorway of the pharmacy across from the pub his guy had just entered. It looked like he wasn't going to be coming out for a while. He had found himself a seat and was gazing at the menu.

Patrick decided that nothing was going to happen tonight, so he decided that food was what he needed as well. He had noticed a little out-of-the-way diner on his way to Connor's trailer and thought he'd give it a try. Patrick took one last glance at the man sitting in front of the pub window, stepped off the curb, and was nearly knocked off his feet by the force of the collision with the person going into the store.

Connor O'Reilly!

How the hell that man always managed to be in his face when he was gathering evidence was beyond him. Maybe he should let O'Reilly in on his motive for being there – but then again, maybe it was too early for that.

"Hey Ryan, where you going in such a hurry?"

Thinking quickly, Patrick said, "Just thought I'd go get something to eat. I heard that Dallas got hurt. How's she doing?"

"She'll be fine. Just a twisted knee and a bump on the head. Could've been a lot worse though, if she wasn't such an excellent rider."

Connor watched Patrick for a reaction. He still wasn't sure what Ryan's game was. He'd done a background check on him just to be safe and knew he was a P.I., but he had no idea, other than racing, what his purpose was at the race.

The two of them would have to sit down and talk *soon*.

"Sounds like you've got a thing for her," Patrick said.

"She's... uh...okay."

"She looks more than okay to me, man." Patrick's interest was evident in his voice.

"Yah, well…" Connor could feel his Irish rising. What was this? Jealousy just because some other guy thinks Dallas is okay?

Quickly changing tactics before he said too much, he replied. "You didn't do too badly in the last leg of the race, Ryan. Did you do anything special to your motorcycle? Soup her up a little?"

"Thanks, man. No, nothing to the bike. It just seemed like everyday there was something going against me – weather, tires going flat, even got lost once – but today every thing seemed to flow nicely. No surprises. So, what exactly happened to her bike?" Patrick changed the subject back to Dallas.

"Someone tampered with it," Connor said, watching for some guilty reaction from Patrick but was just a little surprised when he heard concern in his voice.

"How do you know that someone tampered with it? What happened exactly?"

"The retaining ring on the handlebars was backed off. The longer she bounced over the track, the looser it became until she had no control over her steering. Nearly sent her over a cliff. Only guts and skill kept her from being killed."

It took all of Patrick's control not to show a reaction to that. He and Connor both knew it would take more than ruts and potholes to loosen a retaining ring.

Over a cliff. Over a freaking cliff. His man was changing his MO. He was pushing the limits; now his escapades were becoming deadly.

He was out to kill.

Connor watched the emotions play across Patrick's face and was taken aback when he let out what sounded like a growl, turned, and abruptly walked away leaving Connor staring at his departing back.

CHAPTER 20

CONNER RETURNED TO the trailer just as Dallas was finishing a bowl of chicken noodle soup.

J.T., Connor thought. *He never traveled without an endless supply of chicken noodle soup.* Sometimes Connor wondered if his friend considered it a food group.

Dallas looked better now that she'd had some rest and some of J.T.'s nourishment.

"How's our patient doing?" he asked, setting the bag from the drugstore down on the counter. He had been going to get more aspirins and a better tensor bandage for her ankle when he had walked into Patrick.

"Much better," J.T. said. "But I think she should get some more rest."

"That wouldn't be a bad idea," Connor replied.

"Would you two stop talking like I'm not here? I'm perfectly capable of answering questions. I'm fine. I'm not in pain – well, not much. I'm not tired, *AND* I will be racing in the morning – just in case you were going to ask."

She crossed her arms over her chest in a defiant manner. She wasn't going to budge from her desire to finish the race and apprehend her thief.

"You can't get on a motorcycle tomorrow or any time soon for that matter. The gash on your leg needs to heal and your bike…"

"…is just fine," she interrupted.

"I checked it over thoroughly after I hauled it away from the edge of the cliff. Now if you two are finished playing Florence Nightingale, I'll just be on my way."

Throwing the covers off, Dallas swung her legs over the side of the cot and started to rise. She pushed back a wave of dizziness but didn't get more that halfway up when two powerful hands on her shoulders pushed her back on the bed.

"You're one stubborn woman. Can't hear well either. The doctor said you had to stay in bed for 24 hours because of the concussion."

Connor pulled the covers up under her chin and started ramming the edges in around her body.

Struggling to untangle herself from the confining cocoon, Dallas glared at him. "Let me up, O'Reilly. I can look after myself. AND, I don't have a concussion."

"You're staying right here where I can keep an eye on you." Connor was now practically sitting on top of her holding her down.

"Get you're hands off me, you moron."

In an effort to try and diffuse a situation that was rapidly reaching critical mass, J.T. put his hand on Dallas' now free arm, holding back the punch she was about to land on Connor's arm. J.T. was amazed at the strength he had to use to restrain her.

"Connor's right, Dallas. The doctor said you had to stay where someone could monitor you through the night, and the night is not over yet. I know it's not your own room, but it's just for this one night. I know if you think about it, you'll see it's for your own good."

Dallas and Connor had both turned to stare at J.T. Each had forgotten that he was there.

Dallas was the first to speak. "Look, my grandmother is with me in my trailer, and she can watch me just as well as you. I really appreciate everything you've done so far, but I really need to get back to my own place and reassure her that I'm all right. She's probably heard what happened from someone by now and is frantic with worry."

Dallas had wriggled herself out of the blanket and was bent over trying to tie the laces of her running shoes.

Connor reached out to grab her before she tumbled off the bed, releasing his grip on her arms when she glared at him. But he didn't let go completely. All his emotions were firing at the same time.

Anger.

Concern.

Passion…

Love.

Slowly, his hands moved from her wrists to her shoulders and up the column of her neck to cup her cheeks. His head lowered as his eyes locked on her moist, sensuous lips.

Dallas couldn't look away. Eyes, the colour of glacial ice, deepened in color as his mouth came closer to hers. Her breath caught in anticipation of his touch. An ache curled through her stomach and below. She could feel his breath fanning her face...

"Hey, would you two like me to leave or something?" Like a pail of ice water, J.T.'s voice doused the heat.

Connor's head snapped up, and he scowled at him. Fearing for his life, J.T. backed slowly towards the door.

"Okay, okay. I'm out of here. Carry on. Ah, sorry...guess I should go...bye!"

The door to the trailer snapped shut on J.T.'s retreating figure. Connor and Dallas looked at each other and started to laugh.

Connor brushed a lock of hair off Dallas' forehead, his new favorite habit, and his hand came down to cradle her cheek again. Leaning over he kissed her lightly on the nose.

"I don't know about you, but I'm tired, and if I have to get up every couple of hours to wake you, I'd better get some shut eye."

"Yah, all that...uh...wrestling around made me...um... tired too." Dallas closed her eyes as if to prove her point, but all she could see was Connor's smile.

Connor stood gazing down at her. He knew he'd better leave her alone while he still could. The passion that had flared minutes ago still simmered just below the surface of his restraint. He knew he would be lost if Dallas gave the slightest indication that she wanted to resume what had been so rudely interrupted.

Dallas opened her eyes. Connor was still there. The fire that had flared between them rekindled. All he had to do was look at her, and she wanted him.

"Connor, are you OK?"

"Yes – no. I don't know. I want to let you get some sleep, but I don't want you to. I want..." Conner hesitated.

"What do you want Connor?"

Instead of answering her, he sat back down on the edge of the bed and gathered her into his arms. His mouth came together with hers in a kiss that was savage yet filled with promise. He knew he should be gentle, but when her lips parted and her tongue thrust into his mouth deepening the kiss, all reasonable thought vanished.

Connor knew he should stop, knew he should be the one to break off and let her rest, but God help him, he couldn't. He couldn't get enough of her. Her lush body pressed up against his drove him to the brink. He wanted to be one with her. Be inside her. Make her his own.

Just when he thought he could stand no more, Dallas rolled on her side coming over on top of him, never breaking contact with his lips. With one hand, she pulled open her top, exposing her breasts with their already pearled nipples. Placing her hands on either side of his head, Dallas slowly straightened her arms breaking their kiss but bringing her breasts level with Connor's mouth. He needed no further urging from her. Slowly, he drew the pebbled nipple into the warmth of his mouth.

Dallas almost screamed with the sensation. Hot shafts of pleasure coursed through her, fanning to flame her need to be with this man. Never had she experienced anything so potent, so all consuming. Her mind could focus on only one thing – having Connor inside her. Dallas knew only he could quench her fire.

Connor couldn't control himself. He knew he shouldn't be doing this. She was hurt and needed time to rest and heal. But his body was having none of it. He knew he should take his time, make love to her slowly, but he couldn't. With her moving in rhythm with him, he was losing control.

He wanted her now.

Rolling them back over, Connor trapped Dallas' body between his legs. Through passion-glazed eyes, he looked at her, giving her one last chance to say no. Her answer was clear when she slid her hand down between their heated bodies to free him to her touch.

Connor almost lost the one thing he cherished most – control. Stripping her panties off, he thrust into her. Dallas reared up to meet him crying out his name. "Connor – please, Connor."

Grasping her hands, Connor brought them over her head and then captured her mouth in a bruising kiss. He took all she had to give and more. Together, they reached the apex and plummeted from the peak.

THE NEXT MORNING, it was Dallas who woke first. She was pleasantly surprised to find that the night's activities had relieved her headache and dizziness. She pushed herself up on one elbow and leaned over Connor's sleeping form to study him.

Connor had tempered his professional look to be imposing and intimidating; it went with the job. It was a pleasant surprise to notice in sleep that his features softened, but not to the point of being boyish and innocent.

No. Connor would never be that.

His features softened just enough to show the true Connor. He was gorgeous. Strong and so sure of himself. She placed a feathery kiss on his lips and was startled when his eyes snapped open.

"Hello," she whispered.

"Hello yourself," Connor pulled her on top of him, molding her perfect form to his. He wanted to feel every part of her against his length. His hands massaged her back and the tops of her buttocks.

"Mmm. I could get used to this, Connor. That feels wonderful."

She dragged out the last word and ended it on a moan.

"Yeah me too."

His arousal was quick and obvious. She brought her lips to his.

Just at that moment, J.T. barged into the trailer. "Whoops, bad timing – again."

Dallas didn't really mind the interruption. As much as she would like to continue from where they had left off last night, they really needed to discuss the case and get ready for the day's race.

She used J.T.'s interruption to cool their rising passion.

Pulling herself away and off of Connor, she wrapped a sheet around her body and sat down on the edge of the bed.

"I think I know who tampered with my motorcycle."

"Yah, so do I," Connor replied

"Cross..."

"Morelli..."

They both spoke at the same time.

"What the hell makes you think our guy is Cross? He's harmless," he snapped.

Connor's mind raced back to the report he had received on Cross. Although he'd been around the racing circuit for the same amount of time as Morelli, he didn't have a background as diverse as Morelli's. Morelli had a host of B&Es and had served some hard time, whereas Cross had a few minor scrapes with the law but nothing that would indicate that he was their man.

"Actually, it's a gut feeling," Dallas said.

"Gut feeling? What? Like woman's intuition?" Connor snapped sarcastically. "There's no way it's Cross."

J.T. interrupted. "Just hear her out, Con."

J.T. was interested in what Dallas had to say. He had thought before that there was something not quite right about Cross. His background check revealed a criminal father, who was now dead, but had spent a good portion of his life in jail for just the kind of crime they were investigating.

Alex had been caught once. He'd ripped off a family member; his aunt to be exact. She'd wanted to press charges because the little pre-teen needed to be taught a lesson. But, she hadn't.

Maybe that was Cross' lesson on how never to be caught again.

Dallas waited to see if Connor would actually be interested in her take on the situation. When she saw that he was actually going to keep his mouth shut, she proceeded. "My check on him revealed a shady father, some time in a school for wayward boys for pilfering his auntie's jewels, and he seems to me to be just a little too – nice."

"Nice! Nice! This is your reason for picking Cross as a suspect? You have to have more than that to go on." Connor sounded exasperated.

"Haven't you ever had a gut feeling about a suspect?"

Dallas asked. She knew the answer was yes, but realized that he'd never admit it.

"As an FBI agent, we usually rely on fact, not on some female instinct." Connor was starting to sound downright patronizing.

"You know what, O'Reilly? You're a complete and total ass. You may think that I'm some two-bit, small-town cop, but I've got more investigative instinct in my baby finger than you have in your whole stupid body."

J.T. snickered. He knew most of what Connor was saying was just macho bullshit, but what Dallas had just pointed out might be more to the point than not. As a profiler, he knew nailing a suspect was one part fact and two parts instinct.

"Okay, so who do you think it is, O'Reilly? Obviously, you don't think our guy is Cross." Dallas sneered at Connor.

"You're right, I don't *think* it's Cross. I *know* the Heirloom Bandit is Frank Morelli. He has the past to prove it."

"Don't you think that's a little too obvious?" Dallas pointed out.

"Our perp has gotten away with this for a long time. Frank Morelli doesn't appear to me to be the type of guy who could keep his mouth shut about his exploits for very long, and besides that, he always got caught."

J.T. was impressed. This small-town cop was very good and quite right about Morelli. He also knew if he let this pissing contest go on, the two of them would be at each other's throat for the rest of the day and nothing would be accomplished.

"Why don't you two just set this aside until later. You both need to get to the start line," J.T. reminded them.

Dallas pushed herself away from bed, grabbed her clothes, and walked to the bathroom to get dressed.

"Uh. I think it's a little late for modesty, Dallas. I've already seen the whole package. Remember?" Connor let his anger get the best of him. He had no such modesty as he stood on the opposite side of the bed.

Dallas made a rude gesture with her middle finger.

"Yah, but I haven't," J.T. quipped, hoping to ease some tension but creating more instead.

"Shut up, J.T.," Connor snarled at his friend.

Turning to Dallas, he postulated. "Let's face it, babe, you're out of your league. I've been on the investigating end of more cases than you'll ever see in your lifetime. What makes you think you can figure out who the culprit is on your first case?"

"Through gut feeling no less," he said with a snicker.

"I haven't the foggiest idea why the Agency wanted the locals in this in the first place, but I suggest you stand back and let the big boys take over now."

Connor's condescending attitude made Dallas see red. Bending over and picking up a pillow she tossed it at his head. "You're such an ass. Get the hell out of here!" Each word come out an octave higher as her temper got the better of her.

"You're forgetting where you are, my dear. This is *my* trailer." Connor pointed out that little fact with smugness oozing out of every pore.

"Fine then. I'll leave."

Dallas headed to the door of the trailer, not realizing that the only thing she had on was a sheet.

"You can leave the sheet, my dear. That's mine too."

"Ohh." Whipping the sheet off her body, Dallas angrily

pulled her clothes on in front of both men. J.T stood there with his tongue hanging out. He'd never expected to have his wish come true.

Not bothering with her panties, she stuffed them in her pant's pocket before stomping back to the door and slamming it. She had no idea that her brassier was dangling from the back of her shirt. That was the image that imprinted itself on Connor *and* J.T.'s brains.

DALLAS GRUMBLED ALL the way to her trailer. *Oooh! That stupid, infuriating, pig-headed, arrogant jerk. Where did he get off treating her like a child?*

She knew that she was being overly stubborn, but that was her right. Connor didn't help any by not listening to her and acting as if he'd never once in his career gone on a gut feeling.

Dallas didn't want to admit that she was scared. But she *was* scared knowing that someone tried to hurt her, and yet angry for the same reason. She didn't want to say the word "kill", but she knew in her heart that probably had been the intent.

Throwing her clothes on the floor, she dragged on her spare leather riding pants and jacket. She followed this with her boots and then grabbed her helmet, all the while muttering to herself about what an idiot Connor O'Reilly was.

The words "Connor O'Reilly" and "asshole" were interchangeable, as if they had one in the same meaning. If the anger that was fueling her could only be used to her advantage, then she would come out on top today.

Grams heard Dallas storm into the trailer, but she only got as far as the doorway of her room before she was stopped by the sight of her. All she could do was stand shock still with her mouth hanging open. She'd never seen Dallas so upset. Something besides her accident must have happened. Dallas was so fired up that Grams couldn't get a word in edgewise.

And *that* was so foreign to Grams.

Instead, all she could do was watch her baby-girl crash into the trailer, looking the worse for wear. Dallas sat on the bed and started pulling on her riding clothes, all the while mumbling about how stupid some men were. Grams couldn't help but notice the limp, but she also noticed that Dallas' face didn't reflect pain – just pure, unadulterated anger.

Grams knew immediately what the problem was: The poor girl didn't have an orgasm last night. Why else would she be upset? Why bother with all the fireworks when all you get stuck with was a sparkler?

THE SLAMMING OF the door reverberated off the walls of Connor's trailer. He didn't know whether to laugh or yell. The sight of Dallas' retreating back, brassier dangling from her shirt, had the corners of his mouth lifting, but at the same time, he remembered why she had left.

Man, you are a bright one, he thought. *What is the matter with you?*

You don't treat the woman that you just had wild sex with like a little girl who doesn't know squat. That was beyond chauvinistic.

She is a police officer, for God's sake.

She has a good theory – even though I didn't want to admit it out loud.

Connor mentally kicked himself for letting his male ego get in the way of the job. What was he trying to prove – and to whom? Or was he trying to make himself out to be a big shot by attacking her just because she didn't agree with him on the Morelli thing? Anyone who knew anything about detective work *knew* that gut instinct was what solved the case nine times out of ten.

This one mental brain fart didn't make him a bad cop, not if what he was trying to do was protect his heart from being taken over by this bit of a woman. The realization that the latter was closer to the truth than he liked, hit him like a ton of bricks. Was this the reason why he was always going out of his way to keep her at arm's length?

His stomach dropped to his knees.

Connor flopped down on the battered old couch, resting his head in his hands, threading his fingers through his hair. He didn't like where this train of thought was going. He couldn't possibly be falling for this woman, could he? *Oh hell,* he moaned.

J.T. CHOSE THAT moment to come through the door again. "You'd better hurry, Connor, the race is about to start."

"Yah, yah, I know."

"Look, Con, I know what's eating at you. You were out of line with Dallas. You, of all people, know that investigations rely on fact *and* instinct. If Dallas' idea about Cross is so wrong, then my career choice as a profiler is a bunch of bull because half of what I do relies on instinct. Why not bend a little and listen to why she feels Cross is our guy?"

Connor was pissed that JT. threw what he'd been thinking in his face. It was one thing for *him* to think it, but quite another for his best friend to point it out. Connor was getting pissed off at everyone thinking he was wrong, and they were right. After all, he was the FBI agent with ten year's experience and a ninety-five percent arrest record.

And, that was his ego talking.

"I don't want to talk about this right now. I've got to go."

"Avoiding the issue won't make it go away, Con. You have to discuss it with her sooner or later."

"Then it'll be later." Connor slammed the door on his way out.

J.T. stood there, shaking his head. He didn't know how much more pounding that door could take.

Stubborn jerk.

CHAPTER 21

DAY FOUR OF the race was about to start, and the jumble of emotions that the riders were experiencing ranged from excitement to nerves to down right fear. With more than half the race behind them, the participants knew that from this point on it was push for the win. This was where the men were separated from the boys – or the women, for that matter.

Each rider now knew what he or she had to do to improve their time, who the riders were that didn't pose a problem, and who the ones were to beat.

The sun had come up in a blazing ball of red. It somehow seemed symbolic of the state of mind of the motorcycle racers. They would either go out in a blaze of glory or face the embarrassment of defeat. Already their numbers had diminished by almost half, and that in itself was a sign of how tough this race could be.

The men and women who challenged the courses set out by the NSDE were a proud and competitive group of individuals. It would take a serious mechanical problem or injury to make them even consider the thought of defeat.

The word "quit" was just a step above death.

Case in point, a Canadian rider had missed a sharp turn

on the track the day before and sailed himself and his bike into a lake. For some, this would have effectively ended their race, but he dove repeatedly into the lake until he located his motorcycle and dragged it up on shore. The race was finished for him, but his perseverance was what this race was all about.

Another rider had slept the night before with his boot on so that the ankle he had broken in the previous day's race wouldn't swell. He didn't expect to win; he just wanted to finish the race.

The mood of the racers was one of apprehension – not only for the terrain but also for themselves. They had heard what happened to Dallas Nolan, and they were afraid that someone was taking it upon themselves to eliminate the competition. It seemed whoever it was would stop at nothing, including injuring or even killing their rivals.

Talk around the course ran from worry to fear that the culprit was the same person who had messed with the bike of a racer killed in South America. It didn't matter that the official investigation had concluded that it was an accident. There were still those who didn't believe it for a minute.

All of the racers left in this race would be checking and double-checking their equipment today.

HE STOOD AT *the far end of the start line and was more than a little shocked to see Dallas limp her way up with her bike. He had been sure that her accident would have shaken her up enough to quit.*

He had to admire her moxie, but he needed the sheriff out of his way.

You are one obstinate bitch. You know you don't stand a chance of catching me, *he thought, laughing at the double entendre*. But if you want to give it a shot, go right ahead. I have bigger fish to fry.

CONNOR WAS WATCHING Dallas as well. His concern for her almost overshadowed his common sense. She was proving to be one tough lady, and Connor hoped this would not be her undoing. He wanted to go to her and apologize for their earlier fiasco but knew that this wasn't the time and certainly not the place. Even so, watching her roar off from the start line was the hardest thing he had ever done.

He cast a quick glance at his suspects, and he was concerned by the way one was watching Dallas. Connor would have to watch this one more closely today to make sure that no one got another crack at her.

J.T. was still ragging on Connor as he pushed his bike to the start line. He knew he wouldn't be able to talk to him once Connor was past the check-in point, so he hurried to say his piece.

"Do you know what you're throwing away by insisting that your theory is the only right one?" he reprimanded.

"No, I don't think you do. Man, you are one stupid fool, Con! She is the best thing to come into your life, *ever*, and you're going out of your way to destroy any chance you might have because of your ego."

J.T. was going to get it all said before Connor left the start line. "You know damn well she could be right. In fact, I agree with her. I think Cross is our man." J.T. let that sink in.

"I know we don't have time to discuss why right now. But think about it. Frank Morelli is a small-time thief who just happens to race bikes. He's not our man. You're fooling yourself, Con, if you can't see that. You know me. You know what I do best, and I'm telling you that I believe Cross is our man."

Connor listened to his friend. J.T. was right. He was the best profiler Connor knew, but he still had his doubts.

"Keep your eye on him today. Prove to yourself that *Dallas and I are right.*"

Even though Connor hadn't given Dallas a chance to qualify her reasons for suspecting Cross, he knew deep down J.T. could be right. He hadn't known Dallas long enough to trust that she could come up with a theory about a suspect without something a little more substantial than "a gut feeling" to back it up. It would be interesting to hear her real reasons after today's ride.

"Okay, okay. I get the picture," Connor said throwing up his hands in surrender.

"*But,* I still think Morelli could be our man."

He said this more to himself than to J.T., and that was his ego talking again. Maybe they were right, but he just wasn't willing to throw all *his* evidence out the window because he was outnumbered.

J.T. opened his mouth to say something else, but then the starter gave Connor the signal to go. Starting his bike and revving the engine, he drowned out whatever else J.T. was going to say.

J.T. shook his head. "Man, you are just hopeless. You get an idea in your head, and you don't let go. Stubborn jackass."

All the tension that had tainted the beginning of the day's race was essentially for naught. Nothing untoward happened to anyone or to his or her bike. The day produced beautiful skies, a warm sun, and dry racing conditions.

Although the course wasn't as difficult as some of the others they had run, it had its trials. The hardest part of the race was going to be the motocross at the end of the day. Today, after a full day of riding, everyone was expected to run a twenty lap course of classic motocross.

The motocross course would be the real test of endurance for the riders, who would be exhausted, hungry, and filthy from the trails. Points would be given for the riders who came out on top. These points would be added to the totals each rider had already accumulated in the race, and the winners of the motocross event would receive gold, silver, and bronze medals respectively.

As redundant as it was to do, it was very important to the racers pride.

Dallas was over twenty-five miles into the day's run before her temper eased off. Aside from her run-in with Connor, her focus was on the fact that the day was perfect. This course was the easiest to date, and it allowed her to concentrate on keeping her speed high, her mind alert, and her bike running perfectly.

If Connor thought he was stubborn, he'd met his match.

Dallas knew she was right about Alex. He was their man. Morelli was a nobody. He kept to himself most of the time.

But Mr. Cross, well, he was always in your face. He had to know what was going on with everyone all the time, and he always seemed to have too much money.

Motocross racing wasn't for getting rich. It was a down dirty and sometimes painful hobby. Dallas didn't know any wealthy people who were involved. So, where did all of his money come from? His dossier hadn't revealed any family or personal wealth. In fact, it was the opposite.

Seems Alex Cross owed some big money to some very nasty people.

She would convince Connor that she was right, if it killed him. Her mind at ease, she turned her concentration back to the race. At this point, Dallas was pleased with her run and was actually looking forward to the motocross portion. She knew she would excel there. Motocross had always been her first love, and she knew she was damn good at it.

CHAPTER 22

NOW THAT ALL the remaining riders were in from the main run, they were lining up for the motocross. Connor scanned the riders sitting astride their motorcycles, waiting for the start. Even though the day's ride had been relatively easy, riders were beginning to show the effects of endless bumps, jolts, dust, mud, and stress. This was where the endurance aspect of the race reared its ugly head.

Connor knew how tired he felt, so he could only imagine how the others were fairing. Every entrant and their bike were covered in a layer of dirt. Everyone, including him, was a sick shade of brown.

Some rested their heads on their crossed arms. Others rolled their shoulders trying to relieve the tension. Very few sat ready for the start of ten miles of motocross.

Everyone that is, except Alex Cross. How come he didn't look worn to a frazzle? It was hard to avoid getting dirty in one of these races, but it seemed that Cross was just a little too clean.

Connor's radar went off. Maybe Dallas and J.T. had a point. Something about this guy just wasn't right. He scanned the racers for Morelli and found him looking down and dirty like the rest of the riders.

Ten minutes was all they were given to prepare for this next hurtle. Connor didn't have another minute to think about Alex's appearance or why it bothered him.

"Racers, start your engines," a voice said over the loud speaker.

The line of miserable-looking humans and bikes tried to straighten out and prepare for this last round. Heads slowly lifted. Bodies attempted to straighten up. Minds tried to wrap around the idea of another ten miles of racing when all they really wanted to do was to get a cold drink, inhale something to eat, and fall face down into whatever constituted a bed.

The roar of the engines and gas fumes enveloped them. All thoughts of fatigue, hunger, and despair drifted away as minds focused on the mission ahead.

Yes, a mission. Tired as they were, each rider was still out to be number one. This part of the race wasn't taken lightly but with a sense of pride over one's endurance – all for a little medal and the possibility of the prize money.

After the initial rush of adrenalin had worn off, bodies that had already endured the rigors of the past four days – six hundred miles of relentless pits, potholes, on-road, off-road, bad weather, good weather, injuries, breakdowns, and physical and emotional strain – were starting to bend under the stress. Ten miles of motocross circuit alone was enough to try the expertise of the most accomplished motorcycle rider, but after what they had already been through, this would be the final day for more than a few of the remaining riders.

Connor's back and legs were aching. He felt as if his arms

didn't belong to him. The constant jolt of the moguls coupled with the impact of the motorcycle with the hard-packed ground after landing a jump was taking a toll on him. He could only imagine what it was like for some of the younger, less experienced riders – and Dallas. He caught a brief glimpse of her when he came out of the turn to begin the second loop of the track. Like every other rider, she was covered head to toe in dirt and mud, but from his vantage point it gave him a little prick of pride to realize that she was still riding, still in the race. He knew there would be others that would not be so lucky.

The run for the lead had alternated between Connor, Cross, and Patrick Ryan. Connor kept his attention focused on where everyone was on the track. It seemed to him that Cross had come just a little too close for comfort on a few of his attempts to pass him. Connor knew that any blatant infraction on his part would be an automatic disqualification if an official were to see him. He couldn't believe Cross would be stupid enough to risk that.

He had to assume that these little "near misses" were just miscalculations on Cross' part. However, they did tweak his suspicions about Cross and his possible connection to the underhanded goings-on during the race. Connor would be paying just a bit more attention to Mr. Alex Cross from this point forward, and he was sure that would make Dallas and J.T. happy.

On the final two laps of the course, the lead changed hands three times. Alex, Connor, and Patrick battled it out down to the wire for top honors. In the end, the final outcome was Connor first, Alex second, followed by Patrick. Behind all the backslapping and congratulations, a current of mistrust and suspicion lingered. Concealing their individual thoughts for each other from the assembled audience, they knew at that moment that the next two days would be a test of wills and convictions.

The *three heroes of the day* didn't notice Dallas cross the finish line or the fact that she was all but done in.

They didn't notice her limping to the impound area, pushing her bike too exhausted and sore to ride another minute. All she wanted was a hot shower, food, and sleep. Her grandmother would have to wait to hear about her day, which would not sit well as she was more excited about this damn race than Dallas was. Grams seemed to forget the fact that Dallas was also there to help track down a criminal.

That part didn't seem to interest her grandmother at all.

CHAPTER 23

CONNOR AND J.T. made their way over to the local diner, not caring that they were covered with mud and dead tired. Connor was sick and tired of listening to J.T. tell him how hungry he was.

"Hey Con, you ready for some supper? Of course you are."

J.T. had a habit of asking and answering his own questions. At times Connor wondered whether he realized he was doing it. It was almost like J.T. had a split personality.

"Is that all you can ever think about? Your stomach? You're obsessed about eating."

J.T. rubbed his stomach and wiggled his eyebrows. "Am not. Just a growing boy."

"Yah, right," Connor answered.

The farthest thing from Connor's mind at that moment was eating. He needed a shower and some sleep, but he also needed to go over the details of the latest robbery. Something niggled at the back of his mind, and it was telling him that Dallas might be on to something.

He needed to go over Cross' profile again, but his thoughts were interrupted by another comment from J.T. about how he was growing weaker by the moment. Connor knew the only thing that would shut him up was to feed him.

"Yeah, you'll be growing alright, in all the wrong places."

"Are you insulting my washboard abs there, my friend? I think not." J.T. was no slouch in the physique department, but he didn't hold a candle to Connor.

"This body makes the average woman drool. Stop dead in their tracks. I tell you they just faint at my feet. You're just jealous 'cause you're ugly."

"Yah, I guess the ladies just like me for my uh…personality?" Connor joked.

"What personality?" Oh, you mean your ego."

"Did I ever tell you that you're full of shit?" Connor snapped back.

The two men had been hassling each other in their usual manner the entire walk over. No offense was ever intended and none was ever taken –it came with the territory of friendship.

They walked into the local restaurant ready to pacify J.T.'s hunger and to discuss the case. Once inside, they felt like they had just walked through a time warp. Here was a fifties diner right down to the padded leather booths, the sit-down counter, the jukebox in the corner, and the waitresses in their pink and white, frilly uniforms.

"I don't think we're in Kansas anymore, Con," J.T. commented.

"Yeah, I think you're right, J.T. I wonder whether they still serve root beer floats?"

"Don't know; don't care. I just hope they make a damn good hamburger."

"Me too."

A waitress interrupted them. "Can I help you gents? There's no booths, so you'll have to sit at the counter if you want something to eat."

"No problem," they said in unison. When the waitress returned, Connor ordered for both of them.

"We'll have two of your jumbo burgers, two large fries, and two Coronas."

"Comin' right up." She turned toward the kitchen and bellowed, "Two steers on a platter, two large spuds, and two Mexicans."

Connor and J.T. just shook their heads.

"Dallas should be here any minute, Con. I asked her to join us. I figured after this morning's fireworks it would be a good idea to sit down and hash this out…you know pretend that we're all grown ups."

J.T. let the intended insult fall directly on Connor's shoulders.

"Yah, yah. I want to hear her reasons for Cross being number one on *her* list. I have to admit a few things about him have been bugging me, and I hope that she has something in her research – other than her gut feeling –to give me concrete answers to *my* suspicions."

J.T. stared at Connor in shock; his friend was admitting that he might be wrong. Shit! Where was a video camera when you needed one?

J.T. thought that Dallas had been on the right track from the beginning. Morelli was too, too…stupid to pull off something like this. He was small time, and most likely had followed a leader in his various criminal activities.

The two men were lingering over their burgers and beer when Dallas finally walked in.

"Hey Dallas, over here," J.T. bellowed over the din in the diner.

Dallas walked to the counter and sat down. She'd had every

intention of staying in tonight, but the case wouldn't let her. As much as she didn't relish another run-in with Conner, she had to talk to him about it.

She pinched her nose between her thumb and forefinger. She looked all but done in.

"You still got a headache, Dallas? I told you racing wasn't a good idea today," Connor quipped smugly.

"Bite me, O'Reilly."

"As tempting as that idea is, I think it would be safer all around if we just put our heads together and discussed the case."

Connor's smile indicated to Dallas that the "bite me" part would come later.

"Are we going to discuss this with an open mind this time, O'Reilly?" Dallas enquired sarcastically.

Connor nodded and said, "So, give me your take on why you think it's Cross."

Dallas had brought all her computer printouts with her to the diner. She had planned on working on her theories after her supper, but now that Connor was in an open frame of mind, putting their heads together seemed like a good idea.

"Okay, here's what I've got. The computer kicked out two interesting profiles; Morelli being one of them. I realize where you're coming from, Connor, with your thoughts about him. He does have an extensive rap sheet and it does include break and enter, but what bothers me is that he always gets caught."

She looked at him waiting for a rebuke. When he remained silent, she went on. "I think the poor jerk would get caught jaywalking, he's that obvious. So, I said to myself, 'Can this guy pull off heists like the Heirloom Bandit?' My answer was no. He doesn't have the finesse." When he didn't comment she went on.

"Alex Cross, on the other hand, has a very interesting background. Number one, his father was a world-renowned cat burglar in Europe, or at least that's what the authorities thought. I know you've probably heard stories about the exploits of 'Diamond Jack'. His activities hit the papers in the US back in the eighties. When the authorities were getting too close to learning his identity, he came to the US but it wasn't long before the law caught up to him. What you may not know is that Diamond Jack was Alex's father."

She let that sink in before continuing. "Another interesting fact is that the character known as 'Diamond Jack' never…got…caught."

Dallas said the last three words with long pauses between them for emphasis.

"Wait a minute! How did you get all that information? We've had a background search going into Morelli and Cross's family histories, but so far we've come up dry," Connor snarled.

"Well you know Betty…"

"Don't tell me – she's a computer hacker."

"Well. Sort of. She just has a knack for getting into places that most people fear to tread. Anyway, Scotland Yard's records…"

"You're telling me she hacked into the Scotland Yard data base…?" J.T. stammered.

"Maybe…" Dallas was not about to admit to any wrongdoing on Betty's part.

"But if you'll let me finish, it showed that Alex spent some time with his father before he died. What do you want to bet the old man 'taught him' everything he knew?"

Now it was J.T.'s turn to be impressed. This small-town cop

had big-town balls. "You know, Dallas, if you ever get tired of playing country sheriff, I'll bet the FBI would take you on."

Connor glared at J.T.

Dallas smiled.

"That's not my only reason for suspecting Alex. He throws around money like he's got more than enough to burn, yet his employment record is non-existent. During the last few days, I've tried to keep a close eye on him while we're racing, but I'd lose him very near the beginning of the course. It didn't matter how many racers I passed, I never picked him up again until the latter part of the race."

"Now, I know that doesn't seem too curious, but what if he takes off to case his next hit and then picks up the race with no one the wiser?"

"Pretty much everything you have is circumstantial, Dallas, but I can see where you believe it's Cross over Morelli. I'm going to go back to my trailer and run a couple of more checks on both men. Maybe I'll keep a closer eye on Cross myself."

Connor pushed back his stool and rose to leave. "I'll see you later, J.T." Connor turned to Dallas and gave a slight nod of his head. "Oh! And by the way, not bad, Sheriff – not bad at all."

J.T. and Dallas both stared slack-jawed in amazement.

"Well that went better than I thought it would. You know, Dallas, it takes a lot to win praise from Connor. Congratulations on a job well done."

Dallas and J.T. said goodnight, agreeing they would pick up in the morning.

CHAPTER 24

IT WAS THE end of day five of the NSDE with no significant improvement in Dallas' time, but she didn't care. The headlines in the paper today were ablaze with homes in the previous town being robbed.

Citizens were demanding action. It seemed that some of the towns that the race went through had a rash of break-ins. Homes were invaded, and the law had no leads, or if they did, they weren't sharing.

Dallas caught up with J.T. heading towards his trailer. "Did you see the papers today, J.T.? Seems our man has struck again."

"Yeah, Connor and I were just discussing that. Did you want to join us for supper so that we can put our heads together and see if there are any solid clues confirming that it's Alex."

Dallas shot J.T. a surprised look. "Yeah, I agree with you, Dallas. I'm convinced it's Cross, but we need concrete evidence pointing to him before we make any kind of move."

"I'll be there," she said.

"Tomorrow is the last day, which means it's his last chance to score." "By the way," she said, "I'm going to get a little tipsy tonight, and then I might just mosey on down to his trailer to see if I can find any evidence that will solidify our case against him."

Dallas gave J.T. a wink. She didn't really plan on drinking herself into a stupor, but if Alex were watching, which she knew he would be, he'd think she was hammered.

"You're not serious about this?"

Dallas just shrugged her shoulders.

"Listen, I'll scope his trailer; it's too dangerous for you. If Cross is our man, he's already tried to take you out once. I'm not riding, so that gives me time between checkpoints to get to his trailer, rifle through it, and then meet up with Connor. Alex will be none the wiser."

Dallas knew J.T.'s suggestion made sense, but she really wanted to be the one to make the collar. She didn't know why it was so important. Maybe it was because Connor might still have doubts about her suspicions. She was a good cop, and this was her chance to prove it.

"Let's go hook up with Connor. I know he's starting to come around to our way of thinking…"

"Whoa! What do you mean 'our way of thinking'?" Dallas queried. Up until a few minutes ago, it was *my* way of thinking."

"I've been leaning towards your theory from the beginning, but we have to make sure he's fully on our side. He's the lead investigator, and we have to convince him we're right."

Dallas sighed. "Yah, I know. I'll meet up with you in a few minutes. I have to go back to my trailer and change."

Dallas walked through the trailer door just as Grams came out of the bedroom, slamming the door against the door jam.

"Whoa, hold on there, Grams, where's the fire?"

"Fire, Fire, I don't smell any smoke. What do you mean, Dallas? Are you alright?"

Dallas just shook her head, not wanting to get into it. Trying to explain would take more effort than it was worth.

"I'm fine, Grams. I just came in to change. I'm meeting Connor and J.T. for dinner to discuss the case. Seems that 'God himself', the great Connor O'Reilly, is actually coming around to believing my theory on our suspect. He's beginning to suspect Alex Cross as well."

"Which one is Alex Cross, dear? Not that lovely young man with the wonderful manners?"

"Yah, that would be the one Grams," Dallas quipped.

Manners were a big thing with her grandmother, and it *would be* the only thing she would remember about a possible suspect.

"You know, Dallas, I found it really strange that he would be wearing a signet ring with the emblem of the 'Fighting Tigers'. I mean they were an elite group of fighter pilots that flew during the Second World War."

"How do you know that, Grams?"

"Well you know the lovely Mrs. Ruttabaker…" Grams thought everyone was "lovely".

"…well, her late husband, God rest his soul, wore that very same ring. Seems the surviving members of the team had them specially made to remember their fallen comrades."

Dallas planted a great big kiss on Grams' forehead. "You are a wonder sometimes. Did you know that?"

"Why thank you, dear. You're a wonder too."

Dallas was still laughing as she ran out the door and headed towards the pub. *Wait 'til I slap Mr. O'Reilly with this.*

J.T. and Connor were already seated when Dallas came in. She headed over to their table with a smug smile on her face.

"Somebody owes me a hug. I just cracked our case," Dallas smirked.

"I can cover that," J.T. volunteered as he swept her up in a bear hug.

"Well, well isn't that cozy," Connor growled accusingly.

He regretted his comment the minute it left his mouth, but he'd be damned if he'd apologize. He didn't want to sound like the jealous boyfriend, but couldn't help himself when he saw Dallas in J.T.'s arms.

"Take a pill, Con." J.T was surprised at Connor's apparent jealousy. "*We* need to act like adults so we can discuss this case like professionals."

Both Dallas and Connor were a little sheepish. They had tried to avoid each other since their last encounter and each for the same reason.

"Yah, Connor, take a pill, you're going to need one. I just broke your case for you." Dallas sat down and filled them in on what Grams had told her.

"Okay, so he wears a ring with a WWII insignia on it. So what?" Connor commented unimpressed. He wasn't going to let on that he had no idea what she was getting at.

"Well, if you'd listened to me in the first place and checked the fine print on the Texas robbery like you should have, you'd know that the old man who grappled with his robber was a member of the Fighting Tigers. He told the police at the time that the only thing he wanted back was his signet ring."

"*And* Alex Cross' father was a thief, not a fighter pilot."

Dallas sat back in her chair and folded her arms, smug in her assessment of the evidence.

"Tell me 'Miss Expert Detective', have you seen this ring or are you just going to blindly take the word of an old lady, who we all know could possibly be a brick short of a full load?"

"You know what O'Reilly? You *are* an asshole."

Dallas pushed her chair back with enough force to send it crashing into the wall behind her. Patrons stopped what they were doing, wondering what the commotion was, but Dallas didn't even see them through the red haze that blurred her vision. "Stupid, arrogant, son of a bitch."

J.T. sat there and watched Dallas leave the restaurant. He turned back to Connor shaking his head. "Man, you weren't born stupid. What's your problem? You've had other agents crack a case for you with far less, so this can't just be about your ego."

Connor didn't look up. He didn't say a word. He just sat there.

J.T.'s exit wasn't as dramatic as Dallas', but he did it with enough commotion to have the patrons again focus on the table where Connor now sat alone. Connor knew he had some ass kissing to do.

CHAPTER 25

CONNOR HAD SPENT the last five minutes pacing outside of Dallas' trailer, trying to figure out how much crow he was going to have to eat in order to make up for his totally infantile reaction at the restaurant.

J.T. had been right. It never bothered Connor when one of his own came up with the proof that solved a case, so why had it annoyed him when Dallas did it?

Screwing up his courage he knocked on the door.

"Hi," he said when Dallas opened the door.

"Go to hell, O'Reilly," Dallas greeted in return.

"I deserve that and a lot more, but we have to talk. Can I come in?" He was already pushing his way inside her trailer, but she effectively blocked his entrance by standing in the doorway.

"Please Dallas," Connor implored.

"No. I'm in the middle of something really important right now. I don't think this is a very good time," Dallas said.

"I just want to talk, Dallas."

"Connor, I have nothing to say to you. You've made your thoughts on my opinions perfectly clear. I'm about to make *my* arrest with or without your help so, if you don't mind, get the hell out of my face."

He stared at her for what seemed like a full minute before he pushed open the door and walked in, forcing her to walk backward into the room.

Déjà vu.

She was alarmed by the anger coupled with the passion in his eyes. He kept walking until the back of her knees hit a chair and she fell into it.

"I don't appreciate your high-handed macho tactics, Connor. I said leave."

"Just hear me out. This isn't easy for me to say, but you were right about Cross."

"Yah, I already know that. What makes *you* so sure now?"

"Well, after running the gauntlet of angry restaurant patrons, I went back to the trailer and got on the computer. I requested the information that you already had on the Texas robbery, and you're right, there was a missing ring…"

"Keep swallowing that pill, Connor," Dallas interrupted.

She wasn't going to let him "sweet-talk" her in one fell swoop, and she definitely wasn't going to make it easy.

"If it makes you any happier, I had already changed my mind about Alex Cross before you came into the restaurant. I think he's our man. I guess I was just pissed that you figured it out before I did. I'm sorry, Dallas. I know that my actions were anything but professional."

Connor waited for a reaction. "Well, say something," he demanded.

"I'm thinking," Dallas finally replied.

"Thinking about what?"

"Whether I want to smack you upside the head for being so stubborn or kiss you for apologizing. Which, by the way, was probably the hardest thing you've ever had to do."

Connor bent down, scooped her into his arms, and then sat down in the chair, cradling her body in his lap.

"I haven't been able to stop thinking about how we're going to nail Alex, but I haven't been able to get you off my mind either," Connor admitted.

Lowering his head, his lips softly touched her cheek. She shivered as his voice caressed her ear. Not wanting to admit it, but not being able to deny that she desired this beautiful man, she snuggled into his chest.

She couldn't help her body's reaction to him, and wondered at the gentle pressure of his arms as they encircled her body. She reveled in his warmth and to the sound of his heart beating beneath her cheek. Its pace quickened as she trembled.

Looking up, Dallas saw the same desire reflected in Connor's eyes. No, she didn't think poorly of him for wanting her nor did she feel poorly of herself for wanting him back.

"Kiss me, Connor."

His lips brushed her forehead and then slowly made their way to her mouth; his kisses were the softest of caresses on her cheek. When he reached her lips, the touch he bestowed upon them was gentle and calming. He brought his arms from around her waist to cradle her face as he tipped her head slightly. Connor deepened the kiss. His tongue plunged into her warmth, tasting and leaving him wanting for more.

He ran his tongue over her lips, sliding it over her bottom teeth, and then dipping and mating with her tongue. He opened his eyes when he felt her deepen the kiss. So erotic was the caress, he felt himself instantly harden.

Dallas moaned as she felt his arousal beneath her buttocks, pleased that she had the same effect on him as he did on her. She felt the dampness between her thighs and the slow ache deep in her belly as her desire grew.

With his hands still encompassing her face, he tilted her head back and away from him as he leaned over her, his lips charting a path from her throat down to the cleavage of her breasts. He lifted her so that her legs were straddling his. He could feel the heat radiating from her core. Pressing up into that wicked warmth, he groaned from the ache of sexual tension. Parting the robe she was wearing, he was pleased to find no other barriers to separate them. Pushing the material completely off her body, Connor drew her bottom closer to him even as he was pushing her torso away. He wanted to trail kisses all over her but was content with the spots that he could reach.

Nuzzling her breasts, he stopped to draw a beautiful, pink nipple into his mouth. He could feel it harden to a pointed nub. He then turned to the other breast to devote similar attention.

Dallas tried to hold back the orgasm that was pulsing at the cusp of her womanhood, but she didn't have that kind of control. Moaning as the force of her climax overtook her, Dallas ground herself into Connor's lap.

Not wanting to miss out on her pleasure, Connor pulled one of his arms away from her body. Palming a perfect breast with one hand, he then trailed the other down the line of her belly to her hot core. He inserted a finger into her warmth, and he felt her lose control as she pulsed around him. Connor took her mouth with his as she experienced the last vestige of her climax.

Lips on lips.

Tongue to tongue.

He rode her wave of passion with her to its end.

It wasn't over for Dallas. Still trembling with the force of her orgasm, she reached to undo the front of his jeans. Urging Connor to lift his hips, she slipped them down as far as they needed to go for him to enter her. Cupping his rigid shaft in her hands, Dallas caressed him as he had caressed her.

"Dallas," his voice hissed out her name.

"It has to be now. I can't hold back, love."

Grasping her around the waist, Connor positioned Dallas over his manhood, and without premise, plunged as deeply into her as he could go. She gasped with the sheer force of his movement. Grinding down as he was thrusting up, their bodies met in a fever reaching for release.

Holding on to his shoulders, Dallas rode out the storm of passion with Connor inside her, seeking the same pinnacle of relief and shuddering with rapture as that relief came in huge, insurmountable waves.

Neither of them was able to catch a breath before the next wave hit and pulled them both back into its passionate embrace.

As the waves of passion eased, Connor stood on shaky legs and clasped Dallas beneath her buttocks. He didn't want to break contact with her for even the briefest of moments as he carried her over to the bed. He had every intention on staying the night and being there with her in the morning.

"I was hoping you two are about finished, I could really

use a glass of water right about now or better yet, a good stiff drink," Grams said from the doorway of the bedroom.

"Haven't seen moves like that since your grandpa and I rented that 'pornographic' movie back in the eighties. *Debbie Does Dallas*, I think it was called – pun intended, dear."

Dallas and Connor both groaned in abject embarrassment.

"Grams, not another word, okay. Just get your glass of water."

CHAPTER 26

DALLAS AWOKE THE next morning feeling totally satisfied. Turning onto her side, she regarded the man lying beside her, his face relaxed in slumber. He had been so intense the night before, but he didn't look like he could intimidate anyone right now. Replaying their lovemaking, Dallas' body tingled in response to her graphic memories.

She loved him.

She would never expose herself so completely to someone if she didn't. He had been so giving, so gentle with her. She had felt cherished and loved.

Dallas didn't want to be there when he opened his eyes.

Slowly running her fingers over his soft lips, she felt his breath whisper across their tips. She raised her hand to her mouth and pressed a kiss to them, lightly pressing them back against Connor's lips.

Needing to re-focus her energy, Dallas slowly rose from the bed, dressed, and left Connor sleeping. Walking to the impound, she lay out her plan in her mind: *All I have to do is stay on Mr. Cross's tail. If he's going to try another score before this race is over, I want to be there to catch him in the act.*

The first half of this last day's race was treacherous, so she was going to have to use all her skills just to keep him in her sights. Anxiety pooled in her stomach contributing to the fear she was having about not informing Connor of her plan.

Running her hands over her bike, she checked for any problems that could make or break the success of her plan. Finding nothing obvious, she decided she was good to go. Forcing all thoughts of Connor from her mind, she mapped out her strategy.

Dallas' one thought was: *I have to be the one to trap this rat. I have to prove I can do this.*

Connor woke with the thought of making love to Dallas one more time before they had to leave. Reaching for her warmth, he encountered only emptiness. The spot where she had slept wasn't even warm anymore. Apparently, she had left some time ago.

Disappointed, Connor stretched his arms over his head. The muscles in his chest rippled and his stomach drew taut as he breathed deeply, still able to smell Dallas all around him. He was unsure of the feelings swirling inside of him, but he knew that he wanted her – and wanted to be with her not just physically but emotionally as well.

A less-than-delicate throat clearing interrupted his reverie. "Excuse me, sonny." Grams fairly screamed the greeting. "I didn't wake you, did I?"

Connor moaned. This was becoming a very embarrassing and annoying habit. "No, I was already awake. Is there something I can do for you Mrs. Nolan?"

"Well now, that's an interesting question seeing you're the one occupying my granddaughter's bed," she replied, sounding more than a little annoyed.

"You know, in my day, this would be grounds for a lynchin' or a shot-gun wedding." Gramma Nolan made a big production out of examining her fingernails.

"I'd appreciate any restraint you could muster up, ma'am."

Connor smothered his laugh, knowing any disrespect at this moment could get him tossed out on his ear, and the fact that his clothes were on the floor behind her didn't help. He wasn't in the mood to explain to J.T. why he was walking around naked.

Grams stared skeptically at Connor. "I love that little girl with all my heart. I've been both mother and father to her since her parents died. She is my daughter, my granddaughter, and my best friend. If I find out that you did anything to hurt her, I *will* track you down and shoot you in the… well, you know what I'm saying."

Grams paused for effect.

"Now, get up, get dressed, and get out!"

Gramma Nolan turned on her heel and stormed out of the trailer, slamming the door in her wake.

Connor sat stunned. The breath that he hadn't realized he was holding came out in a rush.

"Yes, ma'am. Remind me never to get on your bad side," he said to no one in particular.

Checking his watch, he saw that he had over an hour to get dressed, eat, and prepare for the last day of the race. He was definitely not looking forward to J.T.'s inquisition when he stepped into their temporary home.

"AND JUST WHERE the hell have you been?" J.T. demanded. "Never mind. I know the answer to that question, and besides, it's none of my business."

Connor smiled to himself. There was J.T. asking and answering his own questions again.

"You're right; it *is* none of your business."

J.T. stared at him for a moment.

"She's good for you, Connor. I hope you can see that."

Connor just nodded in reply. His ass had already been chewed out once today, he didn't need to go through round two.

"Tell you the truth, J.T., I'm worried about her. I think she's up to something, and she's leaving us out of the loop. I think she's out to prove herself, and quite frankly, now's not the time to play the hero."

"She a professional, Con. What happens when you're on a case? You clear your mind and focus. Don't think that Dallas can't do the same. She's strong and smart. She won't put herself in danger."

A little shadow of foreboding sent shivers up J.T.'s spine. He hoped he was right.

"Yeah, I hear you, but I'm still worried about her."

"I know you're worried about her, and I wish I could help, but I can't," J.T. said. "She's a cop just like you, and you're both well trained to do your job. Just go out there and get your man. You know there's enough evidence now, circumstantial though it may be, to bring him in for questioning. It's *you* that has to focus now, Con. We've got to get to the impound and get ready. Suit up and let's go."

J.T. was all business, and that was just what Connor needed at the moment.

"Thanks buddy. Let's go over our plan one more time and make sure we have no holes for Morelli *or Cross* to fall through."

"Right." J.T. nodded. "Try to keep an eye on Morelli to

make sure he doesn't do anything suspicious. We already know Dallas will be sticking to Cross like glue. I just hope she doesn't take any chances."

J.T. prayed that would be the case. He knew if Cross felt threatened in any way, he might take it out on Dallas, and that scared the hell out of him. He trusted that Connor would be totally focused. The last thing a rider wanted was a wandering mind. Missing a jutting rock, sharp turn, or a drop-off could be deadly on this terrain.

He and Connor were as close as brothers, but he was worried about him just the same. Dallas was good but would her desire to succeed make her sloppy?

J.T. sincerely hoped not. If a rider happened to ride off a cliff, no one would know until the end of the race if there were no witnesses.

J.T. spotted Dallas at the start point, geared up, and crouching beside her bike. She looked like she was praying, but J.T. knew she was scoping out Cross. She had her bike parked directly across from his.

"Hey, Dallas," J.T. greeted.

She looked up. "Hi J.T. I was just…checking my tires."

"Yeah, that's what I thought."

J.T. nominated himself for an Oscar for his stoic face and even-toned answer. "Keeping an eye on your suspect is more likely," J.T. mumbled.

Dallas didn't bother to respond. She just shrugged her shoulders.

"Everything looks fine, Dallas. You ready?"

"As ready as I'll ever be, J.T., and I've planned out my run. I think I've got a decent shot if I keep my mind focused."

They both knew she wasn't referring to winning the race.

"Smart lady. You'll do great; just take it easy and be careful. I just finished giving Connor his 'go get 'em speech'. He seemed to be a little distracted though," J.T. commented with a glint in his eye and a wicked grin on his face.

Dallas blushed. "Oh. Yeah. That's great J.T. Where is he? Last time I looked his bike was still at the impound."

"He needed nourishment and focus back at the trailer. He'll be along shortly."

"Focus. I guess that's what we all need today," Dallas agreed.

"I've gotta go. Good luck," J.T. said, giving Dallas a reassuring pat on the back.

"Thanks J.T. Tell Connor to watch his back."

Dallas didn't see Connor standing by his bike. If she had, she would have noticed that he was deep in thought. Connor's head was reeling. He didn't have time for these feelings for Dallas. He had promised himself he would never fall in love again. Giving his head a shake, he walked to the start line. His gaze scanned the rest of the competition. The riders closest to him were Ryan and Cross. The three of them seemed to be the leaders in this pack, but who would finish was a whole other question.

CHAPTER 27

PATRICK FOLDED THE paper. Today's race would be his last chance to get his perp. He had just finished reading about the latest heist pulled off by the Heirloom Bandit. He had succeeded once again in looting a home of precious family treasures – items that could bring at least one hundred thousand dollars if given to the right fence. Patrick mulled over his options. He was no closer to his target now than when he started this race.

He had a good idea who the key was to finding the missing Van Gogh, but his client was becoming impatient. If Patrick didn't come up with the goods soon, he would lose his commission on the retrieval. He knew that Alex Cross' father had heisted the Van Gogh fifty years ago, and it was the only artifact that Patrick hadn't been able to track down from the Goldberg Estate. He deduced that it was because Jack Cross had bequeathed it to his son.

After the race, he planned on following Alex, halfway across the world if he had too, to find the location of that painting. His commission would be well worth the hassle.

Patrick checked his watch. He still had an hour before he had to be at the start line to begin this day's event. He took a few moments to take in the atmosphere of the town. Frisco was like something out of a picture postcard. The quaint main street with its village-like setting brought to mind pictures of a time long gone. The storefronts with their Western styling had obviously been lovingly restored in order to preserve their heritage.

In the center of the street was a town square with the requisite band shell. Any other time, Patrick would have taken the opportunity to enjoy the scenery and get to know the townspeople, but his pre-occupation with the Van Gogh prevented him. Taking a quick glance in the general store window, Patrick stepped off the curb to cross the small alleyway that separated the general store from the drugstore next door. He didn't really notice the voices at first, but some phrase or word pierced his brain. He skidded to a stop on the opposite side of the opening.

Wait a minute! That sounds like Cross' voice, his mind finally registered.

Flattening himself against the brick wall of the drugstore, Patrick slowly edged closer to the entrance to the alley, his hand reaching for the gun inside his jacket.

As a private investigator, he knew better than to walk into a risky situation unprepared. Leaning slightly forward, he strained to hear the conversation taking place just a few feet from where he was standing.

"It's done. It was actually quite easy." This was a voice Patrick didn't recognize.

"Are you sure no one saw you?" That voice, he did recognize. It belonged to Alex Cross.

"Hey, no one ever pays attention to me."

"You'd better be right." Cross' pompous attitude rankled

Patrick. He had to restrain himself from giving away his position. All he could think about was pounding that arrogant jerk to a pulp. But first, he had to find out what Alex was up to. *Then,* he would kick the shit out of him.

"So, the lady cop, what's your beef with her? You can tell me, man. I can keep a secret."

The other voice sounded eager, and this sickened Patrick. Cross' friend sounded like a stupid version of Cross himself.

Alex's reply held a tone of contempt. "Let's just say she's going to have a very, very bad day. By the way, I have a little something for you. Just a small token of my appreciation for all your help." Alex practically gushed with his gratitude.

"Thanks man, I knew you wouldn't forget. Hey! What's this...?" The man replied in shock.

Patrick tried to hear what was happening. No one was speaking. There was the sound of a scuffle, a grunt, and then an echo of running feet.

He knew something wasn't right. Risking exposure, he peered around the edge of the wall. There on the garbage strewn pavement lay the crumpled form of a man. Scanning the area for any sign of the other person, he caught sight of a fleeing figure rounding the corner at the far end of the alley. He thought he saw a light flash off what looked like a knife.

Damn, this is going from bad to worse.

Patrick knew he didn't have a lot of time to spare here. The lady cop could only be Dallas Nolan, and she was probably in big trouble. She had to be warned, but Patrick had to try and catch the fleeing suspect first. Taking off at a dead run, he rounded the corner just in time to see the perp launch himself onto a motorcycle and take off in a shower of gravel.

"Damn, damn, damn," Patrick muttered, pulling up short as a pain shot from his toes to his hip. His leg still wasn't in top form from the beating he took in South America, which was a not-so-gentle reminder of why he was going to pull Cross limb from limb when he caught up to him.

Assessing his options, Patrick decided he didn't stand a chance of catching up to Cross with the head start he had. Pulling his cell phone from his jacket pocket, he dialed 911. It took only a few minutes before he heard the wail of the sirens.

He'd explained to the dispatcher who he was and what had happened. Patrick knew in small towns like this, where the most excitement the local enforcement agency had was the occasional rowdy Saturday night, a call like this would bring them out on the double. Pacing the entrance to the alley, Patrick waited impatiently until the ambulance and police car had screeched to a stop.

"Well now, son, did you actually see this Cross character?"

"Well no, I didn't actually *see* his face, but it sounded like him."

"So, you can't positively identify him. I don't know how ya'll do things in the big city, but here you can't go around arresting innocent people just because their voice sounded familiar, and you *think* they're up to something."

"I heard what they were saying, and the bottom line is somebody is in danger regardless of who the other man was. So, if you're not going to do anything about it, I will!"

"Sorry, but I have to go, Sheriff. Maybe *I* can stop whatever is going to happen."

"Yah, but you gotta sign a statement!"

"Yah, I know."

After giving the sheriff his promise to come into the station to sign it, Patrick took off for the impound area to get his motorcycle. He'd have to fill Connor in on exactly who he was, why he was here, and what was happening.

He knew Connor O'Reilly was an FBI agent. He'd been around long enough to recognize his name. He also knew that Connor must be heading the team investigating the Heirloom Bandit, and he had a suspicion that there was more than just a professional meeting of the minds going on between Dallas and O'Reilly.

If he or O'Reilly didn't get to Dallas before she took off, Patrick knew in his heart that something awful was going to happen to her. Even though he hadn't seen the man, Patrick knew it was Alex Cross that he'd heard in the alley and that he was behind this whole mess.

Patrick caught up to Connor before he left the start line and filled him in on what had taken place in the alley. Connor peeled away from the line almost before the starter gave him the signal to go. He was worried and in no mood to wait. If he didn't get to Dallas before whatever evil deed Cross had planned came to fruition, she could well lose her life this time – that he was sure of.

Connor figured Dallas had about a fifteen-minute head-start, but if he took some chances and cut a few corners, he might be able to catch her. Gunning the engine, he flew along the main street of the town. The stores and the people that had gathered to cheer the racers on were a blur as Connor concentrated on the road. He knew there was a sharp left turn at the end of the city limits that would put them on a dirt road for about fifty-seven miles. It would wind up a gentle slope, taking the riders into the foothills and then putting them on the highway connecting Frisco with Desire, the last stop on the course.

Watching carefully for the marker just before the junction and anticipating his move, Connor began to lean into the turn. The motorcycle responded as if it were an extension of his body, gliding around the curve without so much as disturbing a stone. Years of circuit racing had taught him when to take chances and when to go with the flow. It looked like today was one for chance taking.

All thoughts of winning the race were swept from his mind as he concentrated his thoughts on finding Dallas and Alex. He had to find Dallas first to ensure she was safe and Cross next to arrest his sorry ass.

Patrick decided to help Connor any way he could. He figured that if the two of them kept tabs on Cross, it would narrow the chance of him escaping capture. Patrick also knew that Connor's first thought would be for Dallas' safety. If he could be any help nailing Cross, it would only benefit him in the end for finding the location of the Van Gogh. He knew that if Connor wanted to nail Cross for all his other various crimes, including the latest assault on the guy in the alley, he would have to ride hard and fast to catch up to him.

Throwing caution to the wind, Patrick relied solely on instinct and guts to make up the time. He knew one wrong move on this course could prove disastrous.

Five miles into the course, Patrick realized that the organizers had really underestimated this stretch of terrain. It was far from the easy pace they had indicated on the route maps. Patrick figured he could make up a couple of minutes by going full out, but he still wasn't sure how much farther ahead Alex might be.

That was why he was surprised to see him over the next ridge.

Initially, Alex had a twenty-minute lead, but now it looked like it was down to just a couple of minutes. What had happened?

Not wanting to dwell too long on the *what*, he was just thankful for whatever had slowed Alex down. Patrick knew Cross was directly involved in whatever was going to happen to Dallas, and he assumed that whatever it was hadn't taken place yet, so he still had a chance to stop it.

Squeezing the throttle, he picked up even more speed, determined to catch the bastard. Had he been paying more attention to the terrain instead of his pursuit, he might have noticed the wheel lying off the side of the trail.

CHAPTER 28

AFTER DISPATCHING HIS unwitting helper in the alley, Alex took off when he heard the sounds of someone approaching. Turning back, he was stunned to see who it was. He knew Ryan was in the race, but he thought that South America had done enough damage to Patrick Ryan to keep him from being a threat. Seems he was wrong. He was persistent; he'd give him that. No matter.

He knew there wasn't much he would be able to do about his surprise guest, so he focused on the redhead and the early demise that he had planned for her.

Alex was torn. Should he stay back and watch Dallas' downfall or go for the gold, as they say. This promised to be his best race ever in more ways than one. He knew he was well in the lead and stood a better than great chance of winning, but the thought of watching Dallas go down was more than he could stand. What pleasure it would give him to see that small-town Nancy Drew end up broken and bleeding as Alex sailed past to claim the prize money.

Just the thought gave him overwhelming physical satisfaction.

He had calculated approximately how many miles into the

course it would be when Dallas' troubles would begin and when she would realize that nothing could save her. The vision of the impending "accident" was more than Alex could stand. He had to watch. Had to savor the final defeat of his enemy. How dare a *woman* think she could bring him down.

He first realized that there was a substantial high to watching someone die when his friend in South America was killed. He had stood over him and watched as the life drained from his body. It was almost erotic. Lately, the challenge of pulling off a heist was losing its edge. He had become so good at it that it took no effort or planning. He just knew he could do it, so he decided to find something else to put the thrill back into his life. Yah, he'd still pull off the heists because they funded his lifestyle, but he knew the act of being instrumental in someone's death was where the rush was.

He left the start line on a high. Nothing could bring him down today – nothing. He tried not to think about what was going to happen to the busy-body sheriff but the thought of watching it happen was too much.

Turning around Alex headed back the way he had come. Yes, he had to be there. He had to see the fruits of his labour. The thought of it was almost like a sexual high.

A couple of hard hits and her front wheel would be history. Backing off the lug nuts was just sheer genius. Nobody would suspect that this was anything but bad luck – again.

Hearing a motorcycle approach, Alex bent to inspect some nonexistent problem on his bike. Worry set in when the bike stopped beside him. It was Morelli asking if he needed any help.

"No, no, just a minor problem," he said waving him off.

Checking his watch, Alex noticed that he had been waiting at this spot for over fifteen minutes. That was plenty of time for Dallas to catch up. What was keeping her?

Maybe he had done too good a job. Maybe the sheriff had encountered her misfortune somewhere further back. He thought about backtracking, but he had already wasted too much time. Secure in the knowledge that his devious plan had worked, Alex set off.

He had a race to win.

DALLAS STAYED FAR enough behind Alex to not be conspicuous but close enough to keep an eye on him. She still had an uneasy feeling about today's race. Running through the foothills, Dallas knew her bike was taking a beating. Their current route was rock strewn and slick in some spots because of the bad weather that was forecast to set in. As if nature's elements weren't enough to contend with, Dallas was concerned about the human dangers as well.

Leaning forward, she gunned the engine. She wanted a lift over the next rise. Using all the strength in her upper body, she and the bike went airborne. Landing hard, Dallas heard a sickening crunch and had just enough presence of mind to see her front wheel buckle on impact.

Then without warning, she found herself flying through the air, her hands still gripping the handlebars of the bike as it cartwheeled. She landed hard on her back just off the edge of the path and slid into the dense brush. The bike landed across her legs and upper torso.

She felt her ankle snap; the pain driving into her brain. She tried to catch her breath and realized she couldn't. Dallas knew she was in serious trouble. She could feel the blood flowing from her nose and tasted it in the back of her throat. Looking up, she couldn't see anything but underbrush, leaves, and a boulder the size of a car.

Hopelessness set in when she realized that no one would see her from the road. They could pass right by and never know that she was there. Dallas knew if she stood a chance of being saved, she had to remain conscious. But as the gray haze that clouded her mind turned into black oblivion, she knew that was not to be the case.

PATRICK HADN'T BEEN able to catch up to Cross. He watched as he suddenly gunned his motorcycle and took off toward the finish line. Patrick followed, determined to catch him before he got there.

Alex became aware that Ryan was gaining on him, and he was determined that Patrick was going down...now. He had to ground him before he saw the finish line. Veering into Patrick's bike, he kicked out, trying to push Patrick off balance. He wasn't sure if he could time his actions right, but he had to try. He had to get this guy off his tail, cross the finish line, get his prize money, and get the hell out of this hick town.

Desperation made him successful. Patrick and his bike hit the ground in a shower of dirt and rocks. Laughing hysterically, Alex headed for the finish.

Connor was coming up behind the pair. He saw Patrick slide into the ditch but had no time to stop and help him. He had to stop Cross. His main focus now was making sure that Cross didn't get away. Connor pushed any thoughts of Dallas and where she was to the back of his mind. He couldn't let his personal feelings get in the way. He was an FBI agent, and he had a job to do.

Alex's euphoria was short-lived. Checking over his shoulder, he noticed Connor was gaining on him. He couldn't afford to let O'Reilly catch him. He was too close to accomplishing his goals.

Giving his motorcycle everything it had, Connor pulled up alongside Cross. He swerved in front of Alex in an effort to cut him off and to try to force him off the road.

Alex outmaneuvered him. Veering sharply to the left and gunning the engine, Alex left Connor in his dust.

Connor pulled up alongside Alex again. He quickly glanced over and noticed that the son of a bitch had a knife in his hand. He was cutting in so close that Connor was sure their handlebars were touching.

This guy is an idiot.

What the hell did he think he could accomplish with the knife? Connor was wearing leathers, and there was no way at this speed that Cross would even find a mark. He was convinced that Alex had gone over the edge.

Connor was now even more determined to cross the line first and be there waiting to take the bastard down. He decided that more speed was the key to coming out ahead. Giving the bike more gas, he watched the speedometer soar past one hundred miles an hour. His hands shook with the effort it took to hold the bike steady at that pace.

Alex's psychosis grew. It took him a second to realize that Connor was pulling away. Determined to see the end of his nemesis, Alex followed his lead and set out to stop him.

He would win. He always won.

The two men were in a duel to the finish. Engines roared, pushed to their mechanical limits, tires barely touching the ground. Muscles strained with the effort to keep the machines on the road. Telephone poles, trees, foliage all blended into a colorless blur as the two bikes raced to the finish line.

Neck and neck, it took all their concentration to keep their bikes under control. Pure hatred registered on their faces, radiating a need for an alpha, like two wolves in a pack vying for supremacy.

Man and machine combined into a ferocious battle to the end. There could be only one winner.

Blind rage fogged Alex's mind.

It was Connor who realized the finish line was fast approaching. Spectators' cheers combined with the roar of the engines created an incessant buzz. The crowd of people who had gathered to watch the winner cross the finish line was unaware of the primal combat being played out by the two riders. Cheers became screams of encouragement as first one motorcycle then the other assumed the lead.

With only twenty feet left, Connor pulled ahead by the width of a tire, crossing the finish line first. He knew that if he didn't stop Alex now, he would lose him. Applying his brakes, Connor appeared to lose control of his motorcycle just as Alex passed him. Without enough time to react, Alex's only option was to swerve to avoid a collision. This proved to be his undoing. He went done in a shower of sparks, sliding into the hay bales that lined the finish line.

In the end, it was Connor that came out the victor, in more ways than one. He was off his bike and on Alex in the blink of an eye. In one fluid motion, he hauled the man to his feet, ripped off his helmet, and delivered a stunning right hook to his jaw, knocking Alex back down on top of his bike.

"Where the hell is Dallas?"

By the time Patrick crossed the finish line, all that was left of the altercation between Connor and Alex was the eyewitness accounts of the spectators.

Scanning the crowd, he spotted J.T. standing with the officials. Making his way over, he caught the end of J.T.'s plea, "... You have to send someone back to find her; she could be hurt." J.T. didn't want to think of the other alternative let alone say it out loud.

"Hey man, what's going on? Where's Dallas?" Patrick asked.

J.T. turned at the sound of Patrick's voice, "Something's happened to her. She should have come in by now, and Alex has been babbling about doing her in since they hauled him off to jail."

"Don't worry, we'll find her," Patrick replied. "One of the other riders mentioned seeing a skid mark a few miles back on the dirt track. He didn't think too much of it at the time. He thought maybe someone had lost control and slid out. He told us approximately where it was. We'll get the paramedics and police together to go back to look."

"Can you get along without me for a bit?" Patrick asked. "I'd like to have a little tête-à-tête with our Mr. Cross about some missing art."

"Yah, I think so. We've got the local law to help us out. We'll fill you in later."

J.T. left Patrick to his interrogation and went off to the impound area to find Connor. Connor was just leaving with his bike when J.T. arrived.

"Give me a second, Con. I'll go grab the truck."

"No, we can't afford the time. I'll go on ahead. You follow with the medics. I can make faster time on the bike."

Connor was almost to the point of panic. What if it was too late? What if Dallas was…no he couldn't go there. Gunning the engine, he took off like the demons from hell were on his tail, praying that he would find her in time.

J.T. didn't argue; he ran to the truck and took off after Connor.

He was worried too. His thoughts echoed Connor's. What if they didn't find her, or worse still, they found her and it was too late?

Pushing all thoughts but those of finding Dallas alive to the back of his mind, he reached the junction where the highway met the dirt trail in time to see Connor disappear over the first rise.

Connor had the advantage of knowing the terrain already and was so far ahead of J.T. that he had a hard time keeping track of him. The truck was four-wheel drive, but the road narrowed in some places to the point where J.T. had to slow to a crawl to get through rocky outcrops that Connor shot through like a knife through butter.

Connor was pulling so far ahead that J.T. kept losing sight of him.

God, please don't let us be too late.

Connor knew J.T. was behind him, but he couldn't take the time to wait for him to catch up. He had to find Dallas.

The rider who had noticed the skid mark gave them the general vicinity to start their search. But only slow meticulous searching would find the exact spot. Coming up on the area, Connor brought his bike to a stop. He would go on foot from here.

About fifty feet from where he left his motorcycle, Connor found the broken front wheel. Searching the brush around the area failed to turn up any trace of her.

Panic began to set in. Where was she?

"Dallas, can you hear me," he yelled.

Standing still, he listened for a reply. Nothing.

"Dallas, if you can hear me, answer me. Say something… please."

He listened. Wait. What was that?

J.T. came to a skidding halt beside him. Connor signaled him to be quiet.

"Dallas, please, let me know where you are."

There it was again: a groan, coming from the underbrush on the far side of the road. Running down the embankment, searching as he went, Connor almost missed her.

Her motorcycle and the underbrush obscured her from sight. J.T. came up beside them. Together they lifted the heavy machine off her legs. Dropping down beside her, Connor felt for a pulse.

It was there, strong and steady.

Thank God, he thought, offering up a silent prayer that she was alive. Gently lifting the visor of her helmet, Connor couldn't stop the groan at the sight of the blood that covered her face. Experience told him to leave the helmet on in case there were neck or back injuries. Trying to remove it could compound any problems in that area. Running his hands up her leg from ankle to thigh, it was hard not to miss the fractured bone protruding under the skin.

Next, he felt her stomach for any distention that would indicate internal injury or bleeding. The pressure he exerted on her ribcage earned him a deep groan and a hand weakly pulling his away from the area.

"Broken…ribs."

Her voice was weak and filled with pain.

"Dallas, don't worry. We'll get you out of here. Do you hurt anywhere else? Can you feel your legs? How about your back? Any pain there?" Connor tried his best to sound professional, but with the unshed tears blinding his vision it was impossible.

J.T. came over and knelt on the other side of Dallas, placing his hand on her arm. "The paramedics are on their way. They should be here in a couple of minutes. Hang in there, Dallas. Don't close your eyes, honey, we need to see those beauties."

J.T. and Connor both knew with the extent of her obvious injuries there was a good chance she might have another concussion, and two in the span of a few days was two too many. Keeping her awake and talking would help keep her from slipping into unconsciousness.

Dallas slowly turned her head, bringing J.T. into her field of vision. She didn't let go of Connor's hand. His thumb was making lazy, comforting circles on the back of hers.

"I don't understand what happened. My bike was in top shape…" Dallas sucked in a breath as she tried to sit up. Pain from her ribs shot through her as everything started to fade to gray. Fighting to remain alert, Dallas laid back and closed her eyes. Slowly the swirling gray haze dissipated, and J.T. came back into focus.

"Don't try to talk now. We'll get you to the hospital. We'll discuss what happened later."

CHAPTER 29

PATRICK WAS INFORMED that Dallas had been found. She was badly hurt but alive – thankfully.

The police had finished their report and booked Alex on suspicion of robbery charges. They had taken Patrick's statement about Alex's other nefarious doings and added that to Connor's earlier report.

Patrick had grilled Alex for an hour, but he wouldn't reveal the location of the Van Gogh, so it looked like Patrick's commission was in jeopardy. He left Alex with a promise to return and went to check on Dallas.

As he descended the steps of the police station, he spotted Connor surrounded by a group of his fellow riders all enthusiastically clapping him on the back and giving their praise for his riding prowess, obviously unaware of the injuries to Dallas.

"Congratulations O'Reilly. Nice riding."

"Hey man, congrats, you really know how to pull off a spectacular finish."

"Way to go Connor. What're you going to do with all that money?"

Irritation and the overwhelming urge to punch someone flared inside Connor. He didn't have time for this. Didn't they know he had more important things to do? It was all he could do to stop himself from telling them all to go to hell.

Forcing a smile, he accepted their praise and well wishes and shook hands until he thought he would scream in frustration, all the while edging his way towards escape…he needed to get back to Dallas. Finally, accepting a clap on the back from the last of his "buddies", Connor turned – right into a mass of cameras, lights, and people.

Groaning in irritation, he looked for an avenue of escape. Microphones from local TV and radio stations were thrust in his face. Questions came at him from every direction.

"Who was Connor O'Reilly, and who did he work for?"

"Who was Alex Cross really?"

"Did you think you would pull off a come-from-behind win when you started the race?"

"What do you plan to do next?"

Connor knew he should set the record straight, but he had something more important to do. Telling the media that he had "no comment" at this time but would give them a statement later, he pushed his way through the crowd and headed for the hospital. A few diehard reporters tried to follow but decided against it when Connor turned and gave them his best "back off or die" look.

Works every time, he thought to himself.

The paramedics had stabilized Dallas in the field and transported her to the local hospital. Connor bumped into Patrick at the nurses' station, and both were directed to the emergency waiting room. While they waited for the doctor, Patrick filled Connor in on everything that had happened at the police station and also added his full bio.

"I'm a P.I. I was hired several years ago to find everything that Cross' old man heisted from my client. There's only one thing left – a Van Gogh painting – and I aim to retrieve it before I leave Desire.

"Just let me know if there's anything that I can do to help," Connor said.

Connor looked around. What a depressing place it was to have people wait for loved ones who were brought into emergency. If they weren't upset when they got there, they would be after spending a few minutes here. The once pale-yellow walls had large patches of paint peeled down to the layers beneath.

Some areas showed a green shade reminiscent of the color of vomit and others a shade of institution beige. Cigarette burns and coffee stains marred every surface of the furniture. It was obvious the hospital budget did not extend to trying to ease the pain and suffering of the patients' family and friends.

Patrick watched Connor pace back and forth in front of the window that overlooked the ambulance bay. He jumped a foot when J.T. put his hand on his shoulder.

"How's Dallas doing, Con?"

"Don't sneak up on a person like that. You trying to give me a heart attack?"

"Sorry, I thought you heard me come in. So, how is she?"

Connor looked like he had been dragged through a ringer. Dark circles rimmed his eyes and a shadow of dark stubble covered his chin. J.T. figured *he* didn't look too much better himself.

Connor slumped down in a dark blue chair that had seen better days. Someone had pulled it over by the window, probably in a vain attempt to make the wait a little less daunting.

"She's going to be fine, no thanks to Cross. She has a broken ankle and a couple of cracked ribs. They'll be releasing her in a couple of days."

Patrick told the pair he was sure that it was Alex who had tampered with Dallas and Connor's bikes after overhearing him in the alley.

Connor looked at the floor, trying to suppress the urge to slam his fist into something hard, as thoughts of what could have happened to Dallas flashed through his mind.

"I guess he thought if he could eliminate his competition – professional, legal, and female – he could win the race. He didn't figure on me as part of the equation. Lucky for me."

All three men turned their heads when they heard a screeching from the doorway.

"What the hell did you three do to my granddaughter?" Grams stormed in, her flaming red tights clashing with her purple tube top. Her hair was a riot of burnt curls shooting straight up in to the air.

Jeez, she could scare the shit out of a mugger in a dark alley, J.T. thought.

"Calm down now, Gramma Nolan. Dallas is fine, or she will be, and it wasn't our doing; it was Alex Cross who hurt Dallas." J.T. tried to pacify the eccentric old woman.

"Not that nice young man that Dallas and I were talking about the other night. He was such a well-spoken, clean-cut gentleman," Grams stated, staring pointedly at the three disheveled rogues standing in front of her.

Connor's anger flared at the realization of how well Alex had fooled everyone, especially him. He, of all people, should have seen past the surface. Dallas certainly had, and look where it had gotten her.

The hardest thing for Connor to accept at the moment was the fact that this was entirely his fault.

"That *nice young man* tried to kill your granddaughter," Connor growled.

Gramma Nolan's eyes grew as big as saucers at the intensity of the rage in Connor's voice, but she saw there was something else there besides anger. Was it guilt?

No, she realized – it was love. Connor O'Reilly was in love with her granddaughter, and the fact that he hadn't been there to prevent her from being hurt was killing him.

She walked over to where he stood, hands in his pockets. She barely came up to his shoulders, but at the moment he felt small and beaten. Placing her gnarled hand on his arm she smiled. "You'll be good for her, son. She loves you, you know. She may not realize it yet, but she does." With that said she went and sat down in one of the ratty armchairs.

Gramma Nolan's presence clashed miserably with the drab room, yet somehow it brightened the three men's spirits just a little.

Patrick watched the scene unfold before him. Yah, he could tell that O'Reilly had it bad for Dallas, and the fact that she was hurt ate at him. There was not much else he could do here. It didn't take four people to wait for news of Dallas' condition. If anything changed, they knew where to find him. He had more pressing matters to attend to – like finding that Van Gogh.

Not wanting to bother Connor, Patrick tapped J.T. on the shoulder. "I'm going to see if I can question Cross again about some missing art. If you need me, you know where to find me."

Patrick took his time walking over to the police station. He wanted his anger to simmer just a little longer. People always told him that his anger showed on his face, and they found it intimidating, and he wanted Alex to be downright scared shitless.

After showing the desk sergeant his credentials, he was escorted to the holding cells. Walking down the hallway between the rows of cells, Patrick could hear Alex bragging about being the brains behind all the accidents during the race. He stopped to listen as Alex expounded on his feats to someone in the other cell.

Obviously, these were two of a kind. Patrick could barely contain himself when he heard the other man snicker at the story unfolding.

"The girl was supposed to get it too, but she managed to escape practically unscathed from my set-up for her. Her, I would have liked to see dead. Imagine, a woman thinking she could stop me, when the finest police minds in the country have failed."

Hearing that infuriated Patrick. At that moment, he knew what it felt like to want to kill someone. The lowdown, dirty bastard really had tried to kill her.

He was still sure that the guy he had seen in the alleyway was Cross, but without positive identification, they wouldn't be able to charge the bastard. Even his jailhouse confession wouldn't hold up. A judge or jury would say he was just trying to take credit by bragging himself up. Patrick would need something more concrete to make the attempted murder charge stick.

Cross had gone from petty theft to attempted murder.

Patrick guessed in Cross' case, the old adage that the thrill of his exploits had dulled and he had to add some new excitement to the mix had merit. Theft to murder – *that* was a thrill-getter all right.

Patrick knew he had let his guard down. He had allowed Alex to elude him and get to Dallas' bike. That realization made him even angrier.

"What are ya gonna do, Cross? You said you needed that money to get you out of hock."

"Just you never mind. I'll think of something. A Cross always lands on his feet."

Patrick stopped just out of Alex's line of sight. "Well, *Al*." You didn't really think that *I* would fall for one of your schemes again, did you?"

Alex froze at the sound of that voice.

Turning around to meet his nemesis, he couldn't quite manage to hide the shock of seeing Patrick Ryan standing before him again. *Man, this guy is like a leech. Once he gets hold of you, he never lets go.*

Quickly composing himself, Alex said, "I see I should've had those guys in South America break your arms as well, eh Ryan?"

"Seems that way, doesn't it?"

"So, you think you're a big shot eh, Ryan? You think you've won, don't you? Well guess what? I'll get you back, Ryan, just wait and see. I'll get you back," he ranted. "You'd better grow eyes in the back of your head. You're going to need them. When I get out of here, you're mine. Do you hear me? Mine."

"You know, *Al*, if you get out of here, you can take your best shot. But you know what I think? I think you're going to be in here for a very long time."

Alex lunged towards Patrick, his arms pushing through the bars on the cell, trying desperately to grab a hold of him. But Patrick, not being hampered by the confines of the cell, easily evaded the attack. Quickly grabbing Alex's arms, he pulled him forward. Alex's face made contact with the metal bar with a sickening crack. His nose shattering on impact. Blood blossomed from the deformed remains, and Alex slid slowly to the dirty, scarred floor.

Patrick pulled him closer. "Tell me where the Van Gogh is or I'll break *your* arms."

Alex moaned in pain. "Go to hell, Ryan"

"Not before you. You son of a bitch."

Patrick slowly began pulling Alex's arms through the bars. He could feel the shoulders separating with the strain and watched with pure delight at the play of pain on Alex's face.

"Come on, Cross. Give over, before I dislocate your shoulders. You know I can do it, and you know I'll enjoy it too. Save yourself all this agony, man. All you have to do is tell me where the Van Gogh is."

Patrick applied a little more force. He knew Alex couldn't take much more – and he was right. Alex's left shoulder popped out of the socket, and then he screamed and passed out.

Patrick released Alex's arms and watched as he slid whimpering to the cement floor of the cell.

"Damn."

Patrick called for the guard. "Looks like he tripped."

The look of innocence on Patrick's face didn't fool the

guard, but he let it go. "Guess I'd better go get the doc to take a look at him," he said.

Patrick had no sympathy for the man lying on the floor, clutching his arm, blood flowing from his nose. It amazed him just how far someone would go for money.

It seemed to Patrick that Alex Cross was willing to die for it.

CHAPTER 30

CONNOR, J.T., AND Grams all arrived at the hospital at the same time the next morning. You didn't need the sun to shine when you had Grandma Nolan around. Today it was flamingo-pink stretch pants and a canary-yellow mesh top over a lime-green tank top.

Man, this woman could hurt your eyes, Connor thought to himself.

They stopped at the nurses' station to see how Dallas was doing, and both J.T. and Connor were hard pressed not to laugh out loud at the nurse's expression after catching a look at Grams' outfit of the day.

The nurse looked at the chart. "She had a fairly good night last night. You have to appreciate the amount of pain she's in right now with those cracked ribs and fractured ankle. She's going to have a hard time taking a deep breath for a few weeks. The Demerol she's on should help ease that, but it'll keep her doped up for a while. Her ankle's set. It should heal with no problems. Other than that, she's doing okay."

The nurse smiled encouragingly at the trio of concerned faces.

"When do you think she can leave?" Grams inquired.

"That'll be up to the doctor, but it shouldn't be more than a couple of days," the nurse replied.

Connor was upset by that piece of news. "I don't have a couple of days. I have to leave this afternoon. I've already arranged transport for Cross and myself back to Pueblo – he has to be charged and booked. If it's all right with you, Mrs. Nolan, I'd like to go in and speak with Dallas first. I want to tell her what's happened. She wasn't in any condition yesterday for an explanation about her bike. She's going to have a lot of questions."

Grams wasn't fooled for a minute. She knew why Connor wanted to go into Dallas' room first.

"She needs to hear that you love her, young man. That's the best medicine you can give her."

Connor just nodded his head in Grams' direction. The thought of being in love with Dallas was too new for him to even think about, let alone say out loud.

Dallas turned her head when she heard the door open. She had been expecting Grams but was surprised to see Connor standing there. Even though she had been in pain and a drug-induced haze the previous night, the one thing she couldn't forget was the concern on Connor's face.

Well maybe not concern, more like fear. Fear that she wouldn't survive this?

"Hi," she greeted groggily.

Dallas had a million questions she wanted to ask, but her mind was working faster than her mouth. She knew the drugs were affecting her, but she had to have some answers.

"Did you get Alex? Did he confess? What's happening?"

Connor could tell by the sluggishness of her voice that she

was still under the influence of the pain meds. He wasn't sure how much of this conversation she would remember, but he answered her questions anyway.

Connor explained the events of the past forty-eight hours and Alex's involvement in the whole affair.

"So, I was right then; it was Alex." She smiled sleepily.

"Yeah Sheriff, you were right."

He used her title as a compliment. Connor saw that she was fading.

It was a full minute before she spoke again.

"Don't stop, tell me more."

"Not now. You're tired, Dallas. You're falling asleep in the middle of sentences."

Connor took her hand in his. "Look, I'll stay with you for a few more minutes, but then I have to go. They've almost got Cross patched up, and I'll have to take him back to Pueblo."

"Patched up? Why, what hap...? She drifted off again.

Connor smiled. This was getting ridiculous. She was talking in half sentences because she was so doped up. He wasn't sure whether she was still lucid or not when he bent over and whispered in her ear, "I'll be back as soon as I can. We have a lot to talk about."

He brushed a kiss on her lips. "I love you."

Connor turned and left. *Wow, that wasn't hard at all.*

"I love you too," Dallas whispered but Connor had already gone. It was too bad that she wouldn't remember a damn thing that they had said to one another.

Connor walked back down the hall and filled Grams and J.T. in on Dallas' condition.

"We need to go, J.T." Connor turned to Grams. "I'll be

leaving for Pueblo in an hour. I told Dallas that I would come back. She and I have things to settle."

"You sure as hell do, young man. Make an honest woman out of that young lady in there."

Grams shocked Connor out of his boots by standing up on her tiptoes to brush a kiss across his cheek.

Hell. He was even beginning to love this quirky old bat.

Grams pushed the door open and walked into Dallas' room. She watched her granddaughter for a few moments as she lay sleeping. Taking Dallas' hand, she sat down in the chair beside the bed. "That young man loves you more than he's willing to admit."

She settled herself more comfortably in the hospital chair. It would be a long day, and she planned on staying with Dallas until she was ready to leave the hospital.

CHAPTER 31

DALLAS' RECOVERY WAS progressing better than expected. Her only setback was when the orthopedic surgeon checked her fractured ankle to make sure it was healing properly. He told her he was concerned that it might require surgical intervention. She was relieved when the prognosis came back favorable. She really wasn't looking forward to surgery.

Grams stayed with Dallas throughout the whole ordeal, and for once, her brightly colored clothing and constant chatter did nothing to cheer her up.

She was missing Connor.

Her grandmother had repeatedly reassured her that Connor loved her and would be back as soon as possible, but Dallas was beginning to have her doubts. He hadn't sent flowers or a card or even called to see how she was.

Were these the actions of a man in love? Dallas thought not.

Her forced week at home was not much better. Grams was driving her crazy with her fluffing and coddling. She had to do something besides sit and think. Thinking always brought her back to the same thing: Connor.

"Look honey, I know the waiting is killing you, but you're a cop, you know the procedures. This Alex Cross person was no small-time crook. You told you me yourself he's being charged with assault, attempted murder, and God only knows how many robberies. If Connor is a little short of time because of this, you've got to be patient. You know he'll call when he can."

Grams placed a quick kiss on her forehead. "Now what can I get you for lunch?"

Dallas loved this woman to distraction, and right now was a perfect reason why. Without realizing it, she had made Dallas feel better.

Of course, Connor would be too busy to call. This Alex Cross case was turning out to be bigger than they had anticipated – if what you read in the papers was correct. The rest of the week passed in a slow-motion blur of TV dinners and Grams' incessant chatter.

HER GRANDMOTHER SCREECHED to a stop in front of the sheriff's office, and Dallas made a mental note to have Billy Bob take a look at the brakes on the Desoto. Mrs. Ringwald was on her front lawn watering her flowers. She shook her pudgy little fist at Grams.

"Mrs. Nolan, you know better than to make all that racket around my prize roses. You want them to get neurotic or something? The big flower show's comin' up, and they have to be at their best. Don't you, my darlings," she crooned.

Dallas shook her head. Sometimes she felt like the only normal person in this town.

"Thanks for the ride, Grams. I'll see you at four."

She'd had enough sitting around feeling sorry for herself and wanted to get back to work. She grabbed her crutches out of the back of the car, hobbled up the stairs, and did a double-take at the sign over the door.

"Sheriff Dallas Nolan" it read…and it looked damn good.

Dallas could hear Betty belting out a Reba McEntire tune before she even got the door open. God, it was good to know that some things never changed.

Agent Fuller had kept Dallas abreast of what was going on in the Cross investigation, and she knew they were hitting brick walls as far as getting him to fess up.

Boy, she thought, *all they'd have to do is subject him to one of Betty's five-minute renditions of "Indian Outlaw", and he'd be singing like a bird.*

Dallas' days dragged on in a play of the same-old, same-old. The newspaper articles on the Cross case were dwindling. The phone calls from Agent Fuller had all but stopped, and there was still no word from Connor. Dallas was fast slipping into a blue funk the likes of which she had never experienced before. It was so bad that even Grams couldn't cheer her up with her pithy wit.

As a matter of fact, Grams, the most optimistic person Dallas knew, was getting downright ticked off with Mr. O'Reilly. Ticked off to the point of threatening to do him bodily harm if he ever showed up.

Betty's off-key renditions of the latest in Country and Western was starting to grate on Dallas' nerves, and Jimmy and Ralph were doing their best to thoroughly piss her off. Even Mrs. Ruttabaker's numerous sightings of her dead husband did nothing to lighten Dallas' mood.

Love sucked.

CHAPTER 32

CONNOR HAD NEVER had a more frustrating case in his whole career. Every time they took a step forward, they ended up taking two steps back. He ran his hands through his hair. Holding his head, he placed his elbows on the desk.

This case was fast going from bad to worse. Everyone involved was tired, angry, and frustrated. Nothing was turning out to be concrete. All the evidence Connor and Patrick Ryan thought they had was coming up lies and blind alleys.

Cross was now denying that he had confessed anything to his cellmate in the jail cell in Desire. As a matter of fact, *he* was charging Patrick with assaulting him, dislocating his shoulder, and breaking his nose.

"Shit man, all we've done for the past week is cross over our own tails," Patrick grumbled as he slammed the now cold cup of coffee down on Connor's desk calendar. Patrick mumbled an apology as he swiped haphazardly at the drops in an effort to clean it off.

It probably didn't matter much to Connor. The calendar was dated 1997.

"I don't like being made a fool of, especially by a scum bag like Cross. "My client is chomping at the bit to recover his painting, and stupid me, I had to tell him that we were *this close* to retrieving it." Patrick made a gesture with his thumb and index finger to make his point.

"Now it looks like I'm going to lose my commission as well as my reputation for getting the job done."

Connor listened with half an ear as Patrick rambled on. The trip he had taken to New York had wasted valuable time. It had turned out to be a wild goose chase when the address they had found in Alex's wallet was in the middle of the Hudson River. More importantly, it was the last in a short list of evidence they had against Alex that went south.

Connor looked up when he heard a rap on the door to his office. "Yeah."

A ghost of a smile played around his mouth when Harmony Wells popped her head around the door jam and whispered cautiously, "Is it safe to enter or are you guys still wallowing in your misery?"

Harmony was a rookie FBI agent assigned to the Pueblo office less than twelve months ago, but she was fast proving to be a thorough and dogmatic member of the team. She had been teamed up with Connor as his partner shortly after arriving, and they had meshed as a unit right away. Anyone who saw them together would have thought they meshed in more ways than just business, but that wasn't the case.

She hadn't gone with him to the NSDE because Harmony knew nothing about motorcycles except how to sit behind the guy driving one. All her efforts over the past few weeks had been behind the scenes at head office doing the grunt work.

At first, most of the agents hadn't taken her seriously because of her runway model body and drop-dead gorgeous face. But it hadn't taken long for her to show them that she was a tough no-nonsense agent both in the field and off. Now, when anyone new to the Bureau started to treat her like the flavor of the week, those who had already been on the receiving end of her razor-sharp put-downs, stood back and watched the show. Harmony didn't emasculate her prey, she was too classy for that, but they sure knew who was boss when she was finished with them.

"I think we're finished wallowing; we're up to whining now," Patrick lamented.

"Tell me you've come up with something that we can make stick to our guy. Everything we had has come up a big fat zero. Even the tattoo our victim in Texas saw must have been fake because he sure as hell doesn't have one now."

Connor knew they were grasping at straws and were fast running out of time. Cross' lawyer was already screaming unlawful confinement and demanding that his client be released.

If only Patrick had gotten a good look at the assailant in the alley. They would at least have one credible witness. Instead, all they had was a voice he thought was Alex's, and that wouldn't hold up in court. The guy they had found at the scene was still in a coma, and to top it all off, none of the stolen property had been recovered.

"I don't know if this will make a difference," Harmony stated, "but our elderly victim, Mr. Empringham, has agreed to come to Pueblo to see if he can pick Cross out of a line-up."

"Well, that's more than we had a few minutes ago. Let me know when they have everything in place."

Connor didn't notice the exchange between Harmony and

Patrick, but after a few seconds when she was still standing there, he asked, "Is there something you have to add?"

Harmony turned to face Connor a faint blush tinged her cheeks. "Yah, I'll...uh...get right on that."

Connor stared at the door after she had left. "What the hell was all that about?"

J.T. who had been quietly sitting beside Patrick, looked as baffled as Connor. Patrick just stared nonchalantly at his fingernails.

"Where the hell do we go from here?" J.T. asked.

Connor and Patrick were in the room, but he didn't really expect an answer. All three of them knew they were coming very close to losing their one and only suspect from lack of evidence.

"If we have to let this bastard go, I'll tail him. He'll slip up some time. He has to," Patrick vowed.

"There is no way we are letting this guy get off. He's guilty, and we all know it. Somewhere out there he's made a mistake. We just have to find it. Maybe bringing in the old guy for the line-up will be our ace in the hole."

Connor knew it was a long shot, but it was the only shot they had.

"Well, if we can get the old guy to positively confirm Cross is our guy, that and the signet ring should be enough to get us an arraignment date at least. Without that, he'll walk, and there's not a damn thing we can do about it."

J.T. hated to say it out loud, but he knew it was true. Even his profile of this guy wouldn't hold water if they couldn't get something more concrete.

Connor agreed to go over the evidence they had, just to

make sure they hadn't missed anything. Patrick decided to drive to the hospital and see if there was any change in the condition of their stabbing victim. Right now, he looked like their only connection between Mr. Cross and the robberies – and the attempt on Dallas' life.

J.T. decided to stay in Pueblo to see if he could help Connor. As a profiler, he knew his job was pretty much done, but he wanted to be there in case something cracked open. He knew he was only a consultant on this case, but he didn't want to leave just yet. He would give everyone a couple days and then head home and hope for the best.

Connor was notified that Mr. Empringham had arrived from Houston and was in the line-up room with Agent Fuller. Cross was on his way from lock-up, and the rest of the recruits for the line-up were already in place.

"Tell Fuller I'll be there in two minutes. I've got a call waiting, and the person is insisting on talking to me."

"Federal Agent Connor O'Reilly, FBI, can I help you?"

Connor waited for a reply. "Hello, can I help you?"

Connor knew someone was on the line; he could hear a faint noise in the background. It reminded him of the old grandfather clock his aunt used to have in her hallway – that deep, rhythmic sound that a pendulum makes.

"Look, whoever you are, this is a government agency, and you're wasting my time. If you have something important to say, please do. If not…"

The line went dead. Connor stared at the phone. It wasn't like he had never gotten a weird phone call before, but he had the feeling that this was somehow related to this case. He was having that very same gut feeling that he had berated Dallas for.

Damn! Dallas!

This was the first time in a few days he had thought of her. He made a mental note to call her after the line-up; a mental note that he vowed to follow through on this time. It seemed that something always came up that kept him from making that call.

This case was cursed.

Connor made his way down the hallway to the line-up room. Mr. Empringham was waiting patiently. J.T. and Patrick were there as well.

"Well, Mr. Empringham, in a minute we'll turn off the lights, and you'll see a line-up of men. Take your time, and don't feel pressured. They can't see or hear you. If you want a closer look at any of them, just give us the number of the man, and we'll have him take a step forward. Just let me know when you are ready."

Connor hoped the old guy wouldn't take too long. He had his fingers and toes crossed that he would make a positive I.D., and they would be able to get on with the case.

"I don't need that much time, son. Just bring out the vermin, and I'll take a gander. Still can't believe I was wrong about that tattoo thing, but I'm sure I'll recognize the weasel," Mr. Empringham drawled.

He was a confident man and that made the other three men in the room a little more confident that this was going to work.

Everyone turned to stare at the doorway when they heard someone clearing their throat. "I'm really sorry, Connor, but there's another important phone call for you."

Harmony stood in the doorway, a sheepish look on her

face. She knew Connor hated being interrupted, but the woman on the phone was insistent on speaking with him.

"She says it's really important that she speak to you."

"You talk to her, Harmony, I'm busy right now." Connor turned his back on her, and everyone else followed suit.

"I'll try, but she's really insisting on talking to you. She's even asking for you by name."

"Just TAKE THE CALL, Harmony. I'm busy."

He wanted to get on with the show, and these interruptions were starting to piss him off.

Harmony stood in the doorway for one more second, shrugged her shoulders, and headed to her office to take the call.

Connor reigned in his impatience. He picked up the microphone and barked at the attending agent to bring the line-up suspects into the room.

"Okay, Mr. Empringham, take a good look at all the men."

Connor went through the process of having all the suspects come forward and turn for a full front and side views. The three lawmen didn't realize it, but they all held their breath when Alex Cross took his turn. Connor gave Mr. Empringham ample time to observe each of the men even though it wore on his patience to do so.

"Mr. Empringham, is there anyone you need me to call forward for a second look?"

"Well son, that won't be necessary. I think I can tell you without a shadow of a doubt that the culprit is…"

At that precise moment, Harmony burst through the door.

"What the hell do you want *now*, Harmony?" Connor barked.

Harmony had the decency to look sheepish. "I'm really sorry, Connor, honestly, but that same lady is on the phone and she told me specifically to tell you that she has information regarding the Alex Cross case."

"Why the hell didn't you say that the first time?"

"Because she never told me that the first time. She sounds frantic, Connor. I think you should take the call. It's already forwarded to line three on this phone."

All four men turned to look at the phone with its blinking light indicating a call on hold.

"Special Agent O'Reilly," Connor snapped in to the phone.

"Agent O'Reilly, my name is Mira Cross, and I think I have some information you may want about my husband – Alex Cross."

Connor stood there for two full seconds, letting her statement sink in. Husband? Cross was married? Where was that information on their extensive rap sheet?

"Excuse me, could you repeat that?"

"You heard me correctly, agent. The low-down, snake-in-the-grass, criminal Alex Cross is my *loving* husband."

The word "loving" sounded like a curse on this woman's lips.

"I understand that you have him in custody, and I'm sure you'd be interested to see some of the trinkets my *darling* husband has sent to me through the years. His penance for never being here." She paused briefly.

"I knew the son of a bitch was a creep when I married him. He was never around much, but when he was, all he did was pound on me and then leave again. A week or so later he'd send me a 'gift' to make up for it." She paused again.

"Well, guess what? There's no making up for it anymore. This is payback time."

"You wouldn't happen to have a Van Gogh floating around there anywhere?" Connor quipped.

This woman sounded a little like a crackpot, but he was desperate for more details.

"No, I don't have a Van Gogh, but I have a whole treasure chest full of expensive baubles. Like the five-carat, canary-yellow diamond pendant and matching earrings that apparently belong to some Beverly Hills bimbo."

Connor stood there speechless. He knew that was one of the stolen pieces. "How do I know you're telling me the truth? That piece was described in the papers after the robbery."

"Well, as expensive as it was, the clasp on it doesn't work and *that* wasn't in the papers."

Connor knew this was true from the robbery report. "Where are you calling from?"

He needed to get to her and get all that evidence – if it really existed – to Pueblo as soon as possible.

"Seattle."

She gave him her address, her phone number, and maiden name. The woman sounded bitter but honest. Connor assured her that someone from the Bureau in Seattle would be there to escort her and the baubles to Pueblo.

Connor wrapped up the conversation and called Harmony to quickly issue a couple orders that would get everything rolling in Seattle. Then he turned to Mr. Empringham and apologized for the interruption.

"That's okay, sonny. As I was saying earlier…"

Connor interrupted the older man. "I'm really sorry, sir, but I have to tell my colleagues something before we continue."

Connor turned to Patrick and J.T. and filled them both in on his conversation with Mrs. Alex Cross. Their eyes lit up like Christmas lights. This was exactly what they needed – good solid evidence, if it turned out to be true.

"Well, for Pete's sake, if you'd just let me get my two cents' worth in, I'd have told you five minutes ago that guy there, number four, is the young thief that I caught in my house."

Connor, J.T., and Patrick all turned to see who number four was. Low and behold, it was Mr. Cross.

Bingo on two counts.

"Mr. Empringham, sir, I could kiss you right about now," Connor stated.

"Whoa there, sonny. I'm a ladies' man through and through. Let's just shake on it."

"We'll need to get a full statement from you, and then you'll be free to go until we call you about the court date. You will be back to testify?"

"Yes, I will. Don't let this scoundrel get away, boys."

Giving his assurance he would return, Mr. Empringham left the room.

CHAPTER 33

CONNOR WALKED OUT of the Bureau office that night feeling happy for the first time in weeks. The prospect of losing Alex Cross to the system had eaten away at the whole team, but the positive I.D. from Empringham and the appearance of Mrs. Alex Cross had shed a whole new light on the case.

Cross was now formally booked and awaiting arraignment. Everyone would get their first good night's sleep in days. Connor looked up at the sky. Night had fallen and the heavens were ablaze with stars. J.T. put his hand on Connor's shoulder, "Good night, eh buddy?"

"It is now," Connor replied running his hand along his stubble-covered face.

"You look like something the cat dragged in, Con. When was the last time you were home?"

"I don't know; two…three days ago. You don't look so great yourself, MacKay. I guess we could both use a good meal, a shower, and some sleep. What do you say we grab some pizza, head to my place, and then we can cut cards to see who gets the bathroom first?"

Connor headed for his truck.

"Sounds like a plan, man, but don't you think you should

call Dallas first. You haven't had time to talk to her since you left Desire. I know Fuller said she was recovering, but I for one would like to hear it from her."

Connor thought back to the day he left Desire and the way Dallas had looked lying in that hospital bed – her leg in a cast, bruised and battered, with an IV stuck in her arm. Guilt washed over him, knowing it was his fault she had been hurt. He had gone over all the "what ifs" a thousand times and knew he couldn't have done anything different, but he still blamed himself. It was that guilt that kept him from picking up the phone.

What if she blamed him? What if she wouldn't talk to him? What if, in the cold light of day, she realized she didn't have any feelings for him?

The sting from J.T.'s punch to his arm brought him out of his self-flagellation.

"Hey man, what'd you do that for?" Connor said rubbing his arm.

"Because you just walked past your truck, Connor."

"Boy, I must really be out of it."

J.T. knew that Connor had been deep in thought about Dallas. He also knew better than to talk about it. Connor was wrestling with some pretty strong emotions, and J.T. wasn't about to try to give him advice. Neither man spoke during the drive to Connor's place.

He lost the coin toss for the bathroom when they'd finished their food so, while J.T. sang himself silly in the shower, Connor dialed Dallas' number.

The phone rang – three times, four times, and then her

answering machine kicked in: "This is Sheriff Dallas Nolan. I can't come to the phone right now…"

Connor listened to the whole message before hanging up. He didn't want to leave a message.

He wanted to see her.

He wanted talk to *her*.

CHAPTER 34

DALLAS HOBBLED INTO the office the next morning just in time to see Betty do the last few steps to the latest line-dancing craze. Her singing carried down to the sidewalk, but today Dallas didn't mind. She was becoming resigned to the fact that she might never hear from Connor again. Accepting that put almost everything else into perspective – everything, except that she loved him and missed him beyond imagination.

"Hey Betty, Nashville Records call to sign you up yet?"

"Don't scoff at me. One of these days, someone's gonna walk in that door and say, 'Lady, sign here,' and then ya'll be sorry 'cause you won't have my professional presence to make sure your office runs smoothly."

Betty shook a finger in Dallas' direction. "It'd serve you right too. You shouldn't make fun of me. I may not remember you when I'm rich and famous."

Dallas couldn't help but laugh at the indignation on Betty's face.

"What'd I say? Sheesh, you're sensitive, Betty. I've always thought you had what it takes." Dallas had to hone her acting skills for that little white lie.

Betty gave Dallas her best "stink-eye" impression before

she said, "Ya have a message from that Agent Fuller again. He said to phone him ASAP. Something about the Cross case."

Dallas' heart took a little leap forward. If they had succeeded in charging Alex with his crimes that meant she'd be seeing Connor soon. She wasn't sure she had her feelings that well under control yet. She didn't think she could face him without ranting at him, hitting him, or just plain crying at the sight of him for the pain he had caused her.

"Thanks, Betty."

Dallas grabbed at the pink message slip and walked to her office. Dialing the number, she took a deep breath and tried to get all the butterflies in her belly to settle while she waited for the operator to connect her with Agent Fuller.

"Fuller here."

"Agent Fuller. This is Sheriff Nolan returning your call."

"We got him Dallas," he said, foregoing the formality of her title. "Didn't look like we would do it at first, but we lucked out. Believe it or not, there is a 'Mrs. Alex Cross' with a huge axe to grind. Guess what Mr. Cross sent to his loving wife to make up for his continued absence...all the jewelry he stole." He let that sink in before he continued.

"That wasn't our only break. That old guy from Texas came in and made a positive I.D. from a line-up. So, we're going to need you here by next Wednesday to testify at the arraignment."

"That's great news, Agent Fuller, but what about the attempted murder charges?"

"We still don't have anything concrete to make them stick, but we're working on it."

"Well, I guess what you have is better than nothing at all. It should put him away for a while. I'll make arrangements to be there Wednesday morning."

"That's great, Dallas. I'll arrange to have someone pick you up at the Bureau office and bring you to the courthouse. By the way, how are you feeling? This isn't going to be too much of a strain for you?"

"I'm feeling much better, Agent Fuller. Thanks for asking." She would be perfect if it was Connor asking how she was.

"My ankle is healing. Ribs are still a little sore, but other than that, I'm fine. You don't have to have anyone pick me up. I'll drive myself to the courthouse."

"That's fine then. I guess we'll see you Wednesday."

Dallas walked out of the office and over to Billy Bob's desk just as he shoved the last piece of a sugar-covered jelly donut in his mouth. Billy Bob wouldn't be Billy Bob if he didn't have his face covered in powered sugar.

"I'll be leaving again, BB. They need me in Pueblo to testify against that Alex Cross character."

She watched him dust the powder off of his shirt.

"Does that mean *I* have to go to Mrs. Ruttabaker's alone? You know how I hate going out there by myself. That woman scares the bejezzus outta me. Seeing ghosts and all. She just plain old gives me the creeps."

"Oh, don't be such a whimp. She's already called this week. I don't expect to hear from her again until next week, and I should be back by then." Dallas had her fingers crossed behind her back.

"I'll just be giving my testimony. That won't take long. There really isn't much I can add, other than what our background check came up with and the signet ring that Grams recognized. I should be back by Thursday at the latest. I think you can hold down the fort that long."

"Well, if you think Mrs. Ruttabaker ain't gonna call, I guess I'll be okay."

Dallas' sense of humor must be returning. Mrs. Ruttabaker hadn't called yet this week, so poor Billy Bob might be losing some sleep after all. He always had nightmares about ghosts after visiting her place.

She smiled at him and then grimaced as a sound similar to that of nails on a chalkboard interrupted her thoughts.

"Jeez, Betty. Can't you do that caterwauling at home? You're gonna bust my eardrums one of these days," Billy Bob yelled over to Betty.

"You shut up, Billy Bob. I'm a talented person and don't you forget it. Why, even Dallas herself said I had potential to become famous."

Billy Bob stared skeptically at Dallas. She just put up her hands and shrugged her shoulders. She left the two of them bickering and then headed for home. She wondered whether the office would still be intact when she returned or if the two of them would let it run into the ground while they stood around sniping at one another.

IT TOOK TWO days to get everything set for Alex Cross' arraignment due to the overloaded court schedules, but no one truly minded. Everyone on Connor's team was ecstatic. They had gone from almost losing their man to having an open-and-shut case – at least on the robbery charges. Cross' wife had shown up the day before, hauling a suitcase full of stolen goods, including the necklace with the broken clasp. Connor initially had his doubts that she would show, let alone testify, but it turned out that Mrs. Alex Cross had a vendetta against her husband. And it seemed she had more than just cause.

Mira Cross turned out to be Alex's one mistake. He had fallen head over heels in love with the dark-haired beauty and married her within two weeks of their meeting.

The thrill of marital bliss was short lived though, and Alex soon tired of being "tied down", so he just up and left one night without a word of goodbye. She had no idea where he had gone until six months later when he showed up on her door-step demanding his conjugal rights. Mrs. Cross promptly told him to go to hell. With that, he set out to prove he had already been there and was the spawn of Satan himself. He beat her unmercifully, raped her, and then left – again.

The first of his "forgive me" trinkets arrived a few weeks later with a note apologizing for his "conduct". This cycle continued until she saw Alex's name in the paper connected with the robberies. She knew that this was her way out. With Alex in jail, she would be free of his tyranny.

The arraignment was scheduled to start Wednesday morning at ten. Connor, J.T., Patrick, and Fuller were at the courthouse by nine. Harmony had called to say she would try to be there before the proceedings started, claiming she had some lose ends to tie up.

Fuller had asked everyone to be there early to discuss what was going to happen during the morning with their witnesses. He briefed Mr. Empringham about his testimony while Alex's wife listened.

Connor tuned the conversation out. He knew what was expected from him, so he turned his thoughts to Dallas, hoping he could talk to her when she arrived. He wanted a few minutes with her before they had to testify.

Patrick handed Connor a cup of coffee. "Waiting for Dallas?'

Connor took a sip of the lukewarm brew. "Yah, I want to have a word or two with Sheriff Nolan when she arrives. I don't think she's been fully briefed on the case, so I thought I'd bring her up to speed."

Connor tried to sound as professional as possible, but he knew he wasn't fooling anyone.

Patrick was no fool. He knew there was history between Dallas and Connor, and he also knew that they hadn't been in direct contact since the race. It wasn't his place to ask the particulars, but J.T. had given him a succinct recap of how Connor had ignored Dallas' gut feeling about Alex Cross being their suspect.

He's probably blaming himself for not believing her before she was hurt, Patrick thought. *And he probably wouldn't welcome any advice right now.*

Leaving Connor to his vigil, Patrick went in search of Harmony. He just couldn't seem to get enough of that girl, and if he wasn't mistaken, she felt the same way about him.

J.T. watched Patrick amble down the hallway. "Don't go too far, Ryan. They're about to convene the session," he warned. Patrick waved his acknowledgement.

J.T. was about to go talk to Connor when the bailiff approached to let him know the judge was about to enter the courtroom. "Connor, come on, time to get this show on the road."

"Tell the bailiff we can't start yet. Dallas hasn't arrived, and we need her testimony."

Connor was becoming a little concerned.

"She'll be here – probably got caught in traffic. Let's go, man. We can't keep the judge waiting. The lawyers can leave her till the end if they have to."

J.T. grabbed Connor's arm and pulled him toward the huge oak doors that opened into the courtroom. Connor barely had time to take one last quick look down the hall before the doors closed behind him.

"All rise. The Honorable Judge William Simski presiding. This court is now in session," the bailiff announced.

Judge Simski came through a door at the rear of the bench and walked slowly up the steps to take his seat behind the oak-paneled dais.

"You may be seated."

Connor glanced over his shoulder at the seats behind him hoping to catch a glimpse of Dallas, but she wasn't in the courtroom.

Where the hell was she? He couldn't imagine what could be keeping her.

The judge was calling the lawyers to approach the bench. Connor knew that after a brief synopsis of the charges, he would call all the parties involved in the arrest to give testimony. Dallas had better get here soon.

Connor had just finished his statement and was walking back to his seat when the doors at the rear of the room opened. One of the court officers held the door for her as Dallas maneuvered past the guards on her crutches and approached the bench. She passed Connor just as he sat down, not even glancing in his direction as she approached the bench.

"Your Honor, I'm Dallas Nolan, sheriff of the town of Desire, Colorado, and I'd like to apologize for my late arrival. There was a major traffic accident on the thruway, and it took longer than I anticipated to get here."

Her knees were shaking. If it hadn't been for the support of the crutches under her arms, Dallas probably would have fallen flat on her face. All the advice she'd given herself during the three-hour drive to Pueblo on how to react when she saw Connor had been a waste of time. Nothing could have prepared her for that first glimpse of him after so many weeks.

He looked tired and rundown – and devastatingly handsome. She took a deep breath hoping to calm her fluttering heart. Yes, he still had an effect on her. Why wouldn't he after all they had shared? But she was over him now or so she told herself. And it was obvious by his lack of contact that so was he.

"So noted Sheriff Nolan. You may take a seat in the witness box as the bailiff was just about to call for your statement of the events leading up to the arrest of the defendant Alex Cross."

Dallas was quickly sworn in and took a seat. She related her story briefly but succinctly, never once looking in Connor's direction. After a few questions of clarification from both lawyers, she was dismissed and quietly left the courtroom. She could feel Connor's eyes on her as she walked down the aisle between the rows of seats, and it took all of her will power not to turn in his direction or acknowledge his presence.

Why should she make the move? He was the one who had left her.

Dallas went in search of the lady's room. She needed to

calm her nerves and put some distance between herself and Connor. She knew she would have to acknowledge him at some point. She couldn't just ignore him after all they'd been through to bring Alex to trial, but she needed time to recover from that first sight of him after all these weeks. She was bound and determined to be as detached and professional as she could manage.

Connor heaved a sigh of relief when he saw Dallas enter the courtroom. *At least she's okay.*

He had sat there for the last twenty minutes imagining all manner of horrible things that could have happened to her on the way to Pueblo, but now that he knew she was safe, he couldn't wait to speak to her.

She looked a lot better than she had when he had left her in the hospital room with his promise to return. He had meant to call a dozen different times since then, but something always came up. Then the push to tie up all the loose ends on the Cross case left no time.

The night he had listened to her voice on her answering machine, he realized that too much time had passed to talk over the phone. He had to do it in person.

Connor listened as she gave her substantiation of the case. Dallas was concise and very thorough in her description of the events leading up to and surrounding Alex's arrest. He also realized, while she was being cross-examined, that this was the first time he had seen her in uniform. He had to admit that she looked damned good in it.

J.T. tapped Connor on the shoulder. "Well, looks like we've got our boy on robbery charges. Too bad we don't have concrete evidence to nail him for the attempted murder of Dallas and the guy in the alley. I know it's not exactly what we were going for, but Mr. Cross can expect to do some hard time just the same."

"I can't get excited about five years in a minimum-security lock up when he should be doing twenty-five to life."

The judge ordered Alex remanded to the county jail to await sentencing on the robbery charges.

"This court is adjourned until the twentieth of October."

Everyone stood as the judge left the room. Connor and J.T. made their way to the corridor outside where they met up with Patrick and Agent Fuller.

"Looks like your boy is going down, Connor," Patrick said by way of congratulations. "Now if I can only come up with some idea where he hid that Van Gogh, I'd be a happy man."

Connor couldn't bring himself to share in everyone's acceptance of the outcome of the hearing. Alex Cross had attempted cold-blooded murder, and Connor was going to do everything in his power to try to prove that.

But first he had to find Dallas.

The media had been denied access to the proceedings because the larger of the two courtrooms was under renovation, and there just wasn't enough space in the smaller one to accommodate more than a handful of people. So, when the doors opened and the participants started to file out, the news hounds descended like a cloud of locusts.

Agent Fuller along with Connor and J.T. found themselves engulfed in a sea of microphones, TV cameras, and overzealous news people.

"Agent Fuller, Agent Fuller, James Fletcher of the Pueblo News." Fuller barely missed having his front teeth knocked out when the pushy reporter shoved his microphone between two TV cameras focused on the group of men.

"Can you tell us? Will Alex Cross be tried for attempted murder at some future date or are you happy with the robbery charges?"

Before Fuller could answer, another microphone was shoved in their direction. "Agent O'Reilly, Sarah Reynolds KBCO-TV. I understand that you were following a different suspect than the sheriff in Desire when she was almost killed. Why was that?"

Connor had long ago stopped wondering how reporters got a hold of information that was not part of the public record, but this question came out of left field. He stiffened at the innuendo that he was responsible for Dallas being hurt and glared at the woman who had made the accusation.

"During our investigation we had a list of possible suspects." Connor wasn't about to tell her that list only contained the names of two people.

"In order to expedite the investigation, Sheriff Nolan and I decided to save time by splitting that list, each of us following up leads on our particular suspects."

"So, while you were off chasing the wrong guy, Sheriff Nolan was almost killed by the real criminal. Doesn't really set the FBI in a very good light does it, Agent O'Reilly?"

Connor had never once in his life ever considered doing physical harm to a woman, but in the case of this lead anchor wannabe, he was willing to make an exception.

He took a step closer to the woman but Fuller stepped between them before Connor could follow through with his action.

"Ladies and gentlemen, the Bureau will be issuing a formal statement in approximately forty-five minutes. All your questions will be answered at that time. Now if you'll excuse us, the security team will escort you to the press room."

J.T. gave Fuller a pat on the back. "Good timing, man. I thought Connor was about to shove that little lady's microphone where the sun don't shine."

"Trust me, if we had have been anywhere else, I probably would have let him. That piranha has the reputation of being a ball-buster, but one of these days she's going to push someone just a little too far, and you know what? I want to be there when it happens."

Connor was fuming. The last thing he needed right now was some smart ass fueling his guilt.

He was already concerned that he hadn't seen Dallas since she left the court after her testimony. He scanned the corridor in an attempt to find her. He finally saw her sitting on a bench a discreet distance from the throng of reporters. Relief, that she had escaped the media feeding frenzy made him feel better. Connor pushed his way through the crowd in an effort to reach her.

"Connor! Connor – wait up! I've got news, and you're not going to believe it." Harmony grabbed his arm and spun Connor around to face her, putting his back to Dallas.

"Can't it wait, Harmony?"

"No, Connor, it can't."

She lowered her voice so that none of the reporters lingering within earshot would overhear what she was about to tell Connor. "I just got off the phone with the hospital. The doctor who's been looking after our stabbing victim called my cell to tell me that his patient has regained consciousness."

She paused for effect.

"*And,* you'll never guess what the first thing he asked for was."

Connor was trying not to be irritated because the last thing he wanted to do was play twenty questions with Harmony. "Just get to the point, Harm," he snapped, his patience wearing thin.

If Harmony was surprised by his surliness, she had the good grace not to show it. She knew what a strain he had been under – they had all been under – and J.T. had filled her in with the details about his relationship with Sheriff Nolan.

"He asked for a lawyer, Connor, and then for the police. Seems he didn't want to be the only one accused of trying to kill a cop."

Connor grabbed Harmony by the arms and hauled her up on her tiptoes – not an easy thing to do to someone who was five foot ten. His annoyance and irritation frightened her.

"And what did he tell them, *Harmony*?"

She knew better than to bait him now. "Well now, it's like this. Seems a guy by the name of Cross hired him to slip into the motorcycle impound area at the NSDE one evening and back off the lug nuts on the front wheel of a black Yamaha TW200."

Connor's eyes narrowed.

"Cross told the guy he wanted the 'bitch cop' dead. But it seems when our accomplice went to collect his reward from Mr. Cross – he decided to renege on the deal."

"When our boy threatened to go to the authorities if he

didn't receive his money, Mr. Cross pulled out a very large knife and stabbed the poor saboteur in the chest."

Connor loosened his grip on Harmony's arms and let her drop none to gently to the floor. Unable to control his enthusiasm, he let out a whoop, punching the air with his fist.

"We've got him, Harm. We've got him. Get a guard on his room. I don't want to take any chances here."

The smile on Connor's face said it all.

"Already done boss."

Harmony was so caught up in Connor's fervor she threw her arms around his neck and gave him a long kiss on the lips.

CHAPTER 35

DALLAS KNEW THE minute Connor had exited the courtroom. It was an awareness attributed to people who were acutely in tune with one another. She turned in the direction of the doors and wasn't surprised to see the throng of reporters descend on Agent Fuller and his men. This had been a well-publicized case, and the feeding frenzy was on to see what station or newspaper would get the scoop.

The crush of bodies and cameras around the trio was enormous. People were firing questions at them left and right, but Dallas was focused on only one person in that crowd – Connor.

He was a commanding presence standing inches above almost everyone, answering his or her questions with unwavering professionalism. He looked tired, she thought, almost as tired as she felt. It was obvious he was annoyed, but Dallas couldn't be sure if it was because of what had transpired during the trial, the reporters, or something much deeper.

The minute Connor spotted her, Dallas felt as if the air had become too thick to breathe. He made eye contact and gave a barely discernable nod of his head. Dallas tried to smile and tried to act as if he hadn't just knocked the air from her lungs.

She couldn't breathe.

Couldn't move.

The force of the revelation that invaded her heart was too overwhelming – she loved him. The force hit Dallas like a wrecker's ball. After all the soul-searching, all the well-rehearsed words she had memorized in order to ease the transition from lovers to friends, she still loved him. She loved this man more than life itself, and she would never settle for anything less than having him with her forever.

She watched him. Time and space slowed to a crawl. The noise of the newsmongers clambering for their byline faded to a barely audible whisper. The movement of the crowd stilled. It was as if everyone in that corridor had ceased to exist save for the two of them.

God, what am I going to do?

Dallas tried to focus.

A particularly obnoxious reporter had Connor cornered. She could feel Connor's anger radiating across the hallway. His face was a barely contained mask of fury. She wondered what she had said that had Connor so obviously upset. Dallas knew it had something to do with the case and would have had no sympathy for the woman if Connor chose to let go with the full force of his rage.

Lucky for the reporter, Agent Fuller skillfully defused the situation, saving the femme fatale from certain bodily harm.

Connor turned toward Dallas. Her heart leaped into her throat. *It's time.*

She reached for her crutches. She wanted to be on her feet, so to speak, when she confronted Connor. She noticed the nervous smile that curved the corners of Connor's mouth.

Dallas couldn't help but take in the fullness of his lips, the soft rounded lines. Her insides tightened at the thought of running the tip of her tongue along their length.

Connor tilted his head slightly to the side deepening his smile. Had he guessed where her thoughts were?

Dallas tried to keep her expression blank. She was not going to have this conversation wearing her heart on her sleeve, she thought. If this was to be a re-affirmation of their feelings for one another, *then* she would let her emotions burst forth.

But if it was goodbye, she would do it with as much dignity as she could muster.

Twenty feet was all that separated them when Dallas' world came crashing down around her. The beautiful, young woman who had run after Connor and literally leaped into his arms was now draped around Connor's neck giving him a very passionate kiss.

But that wasn't what made the scene so devastating to watch. No, it was the fact that it appeared to Dallas that she was accustomed to being in that position.

Connor as well, seemed to be enjoying the moment.

Was this woman the reason she hadn't heard from Connor since the day after her accident? Had she been in the picture all along? His girlfriend or worse – his wife?

She watched as Connor smiled down at the woman, whispered something in her ear, and then whirled her around in an obviously intimate way. It was quite apparent that he had forgotten that Dallas was even there. He didn't even look over to see if she had witnessed the embrace.

Tears burned the backs of her eyes. *Please not here, not now. I will not let him see me cry.*

Dallas turned so abruptly she ran into a man coming out of

the door beside her and almost went down on her face. *Great, all I need is to make a bigger fool of myself.*

"Are you okay, miss?"

Dallas looked at the man who had just saved her from a very nasty fall as if he'd grown wings.

"Can I get you anything? Here, let me help you to a seat."

Dallas shook off his hands. "No, uh, I have to get out of here. I mean, I need some air, I'm fine really. Just let me get outside. I'll be fine."

But Dallas knew she would never be okay again. She knew she had to get away from here; away from the scene she had just witnessed.

Away from Connor.

If she could just make it to the elevator, then she could get to her car and drive back to her nice, quiet, little town of Desire and try to put the pieces of her shattered heart back together.

"Dallas wait! Where are you going? We need to talk."

She heard Connor calling to her, but Dallas didn't turn around. She didn't even slow her stride. The tears she had tried to hold at bay streamed down her cheeks. The doors closed behind her just as Connor reached the elevator.

Connor banged his fist on the elevator in frustration. "Damn it."

J.T. and Harmony were right on his heels. "Take the stairs, Connor. You have to go after her. You have to tell her that what she saw wasn't what it seemed to be. Go man, *now.*"

J.T. gave Connor a shove. He bolted down the hall, wrenched open the stairwell door, and took the stairs two at a time to the first floor. Apologizing to a group of startled women when he pushed through the door to the street, he ran down the concrete steps and into the parking lot.

Where is she? She's on crutches. How fast can she move?

Connor looked back toward the doors of the courthouse. Maybe she hadn't made it down the elevator yet. Seconds passed, but no one exited the building. Scanning the parking lot, Connor caught sight of the SUV he had seen parked in front of the Desire sheriff's office. It was pulling out into traffic at the other end of the lot.

He had missed her.

Harmony skidded to a stop beside him. "I'm so sorry, Connor. This is all my fault. I was just so caught up in the news about Cross, I just reacted. I'm really sorry. If there's anything I can do to smooth it over…"

"It's not your fault, Harm. It's mine. I should have talked to Dallas sooner, but things just kept getting in the way." Connor ran his hand roughly through his hair.

"Harm, tell Fuller I'm taking a few days leave."

"What will I say is the reason?"

"I don't care what you tell him – tell him I'm sick or something."

You're sick all right, she thought. *Lovesick.*

Connor went back to his apartment and grabbed an overnight bag. All he had to do was find Dallas and explain what had happened when Harmony had jumped in his arms and kissed him. That the beautiful, sexy woman was an FBI agent and his partner. That she was only overcome by the fact that they had finally gotten a break with the attempted murder charge against Cross. She was merely just caught up in the moment.

Yah, right, like she was going to believe that.

Shit! This was going to take some fancy talking.

CHAPTER 36

CONNOR ARRIVED IN Desire just before six that evening and was relieved to see the lights still on in the sheriff's office. He pulled up to the curb not even bothering to turn off the engine of his truck and ran up the steps. Betty was at her desk typing away in time to an Alan Jackson song that was blaring from the radio.

"Where's Dallas? I need to talk to her right now."

"Well, howdy to you too, Mr. FBI man." Betty didn't even break the rhythm of her typing.

"Sorry, Betty, but I need to speak with Dallas right now; it's really important."

"Well that's going to be just a little difficult seeing as she isn't here."

Connor's reign on his patience was fast slipping away. "Where is she Betty?"

Betty knew by the tone of his voice that it was time to stop goading him and be straight. She stopped typing and turned towards Mister Gorgeous.

"She called about an hour ago and said she was taking some more time off because her ankle was botherin' her. That

I should get Billy Bob and Ralph to look after things for a few days, and she'd call when she was comin' back."

"Did she say where she was going? Is she at home?"

"I don't think so."

Betty stared at the wall behind Connor, deep in thought.

"Nope – she didn't say where she was going to be. I know it wasn't at home 'cause she asked me to call Grandma Nolan and tell her she was fixin' to take a little time off. Guess she didn't want Grams to worry."

The blow from Connor's fist sent the pencils in Betty's "I love country" coffee cup skittering off the sides of her desk.

"If you hear from her, tell her I really need to talk to her."

Connor didn't apologize for his show of anger; he just turned and left. *Damn that woman, where could she have gone?*

He had to find her. *Where to look?* Connor was so absorbed in thought that it took him a second to realize that someone was standing with his foot on the bumper of his truck.

"Hey, what do you think you're doing, man?"

Ralph Tewlittle looked up from his task. "Is this your truck, Agent O'Reilly?"

"Yah, why?"

"Well, you're parked in a 'No Parking' zone," he said, handing him the ticket he had just finished writing.

CHAPTER 37

CONNOR TRIED FOR a week to contact Dallas, but she never returned any of his calls. When he spoke to Betty, she insisted that Dallas was still away nursing her injuries. It became quite obvious to Connor that Dallas was not going to give him a chance to explain what had happened at the courthouse, so he might as well give up trying.

Connor threw himself into his work, hoping that long hours and exhaustion would banish thoughts of Dallas from his mind. It worked – until fatigue had him falling into fitful sleep. Sleep was the only time he could not keep his thoughts from returning to her.

The feel of her lips on his. Their bodies entwined in passion. Skin heated, as they soared towards that ultimate peak.

Connor always awoke from these dreams aroused, unsatisfied, and craving more.

Why was she being so stubborn? Didn't she know he loved her?

He had tried to talk to her. Tried to explain. She just wasn't willing to listen. Connor didn't know what else to do. He knew there would never be another woman who would move him to feel what he did for Dallas, so he resigned himself to the fact that it was over. He would try to put his life back together the best he could and go on without her – but it hurt.

Harmony was worried. Connor was becoming more reclusive and surlier by the day. He rarely slept, hardly ate, and was beginning to look like one the homeless people who frequented the back alleys of Pueblo.

She'd talked to Patrick about her concerns on one of their recent dates, but he wasn't willing to step into something as delicate as a lover's dispute.

J.T. wasn't much more help, but at least he had tried talking to Connor with no apparent results.

She just couldn't see her partner, a man she respected, lose everything over something that was her fault. It was time to take matters into her own hands.

HARMONY STOOD OUTSIDE the sheriff's office in Desire admiring the quaint old building. She wouldn't mind working here. It was a beautiful, quiet town. Probably nothing too stressful happened.

Yah, it would be nice.

She was stalling.

Come on girl, you've got a mission to complete.

Steeling herself for the encounter to come, she walked up to the reception desk.

"Is Sheriff Nolan here? I'd like to speak to her, please."

The man behind the desk was reed-thin and gangly. His mousy brown hair stood out along the side of his hat, making him look a little like a scarecrow.

"Can I tell her who's calling?"

"She doesn't know me. Deputy Tewlittle, is it?"

Harmony figured if she played to his male ego, he wouldn't ask too many questions.

"Yes ma'am, and your name is?"

"Harmony. Harmony Lane."

"That's a right pretty name for a right pretty girl. Can I tell her what it's about?"

Okay, that was enough ego stroking. "I'm Special Agent Harmony Lane," she said flashing her badge. "And it's an FBI matter."

"Well, why didn't you say so? If you'll follow me, I'll take you down to see the sheriff."

He turned to face her when they reached the door to Dallas' office. "If you're goin' to be in town for a while, I'd be pleased to show you around."

Harmony just stared at the door. "I'm afraid I'll be leaving as soon as I finish speaking with Sheriff Nolan, but thanks anyway."

Harmony waited until he had returned to the desk before she knocked. It wouldn't look good if the sheriff threw her out while the deputy was watching.

"Ralph, for heavens sake, you know you don't have to kn…"

"Sorry Sheriff, it's not Ralph. My name is Harmony Lane, and I think you and I have to have a talk."

CHAPTER 38

DALLAS WATCHED THE muscles of his back and arms tense as he tightened the nuts on the wheel. She yearned to feel the smoothness of his skin and the power of those arms wrapped around her. It was all she could do to force herself to play out the role she had planned for this meeting.

Gathering her nerve, she walked quietly up behind him.

Connor was crouched beside the beautifully restored, chrome-covered vintage Harley Davidson. It was the same bike Dallas had very nearly destroyed when they first met. He was adding the last of the custom chrome lug nuts to the front wheel, totally unaware that someone was watching him.

Connor's mind wasn't on his work. It was on Dallas. His thoughts had drifted to her again and again, just as they had everyday since he had begun his not-too-subtly suggested time off.

Fuller hadn't even given him a choice. "Look Connor, everyone is complaining about your attitude, your surliness, not to mention your lack of hygiene. I think it would be a good idea if you took your vacation time early to try and get yourself back in the groove."

Connor had argued that what he needed was to work.

In the end Fuller had won out.

"I'm not asking you, O'Reilly. I'm telling you. Either you take some time off or you can hand in your badge. Take your pick."

Connor wasn't sure he was serious, but he wasn't about to put it to the test. Reluctantly he agreed to take two weeks leave, claiming he had to repair the damaged Harley anyway and now was as good a time as any.

He could use the peace and quiet.

J.T. told Connor when he was ready to tackle the repairs to the bike, he could use one of the bays at the bike shop. Connor reluctantly agreed to return to Desire – maybe because deep down inside he hoped he would get to see Dallas one last time.

Connor never suspected that it would become an opportunity for J.T. to be on his case every day. Suggesting, cajoling, coercing, threatening but finally surrendering to Connor's pigheadedness about reconciling with Dallas.

Connor knew there was no way she wanted to talk to him. He knew because he had tried repeatedly for days to get her to answer his calls.

She was being pigheaded – just like she had been about Alex Cross being their culprit. Once she got a bee in her bonnet, she just wouldn't listen to reason. How many times had he picked up the phone to call?

The same number of times that he had put it down.

Man, you are one dumb SOB.

Connor ran his fingers through his hair for the umpteenth time. What did he care that she had never tried to contact him either? She had never wanted to listen to the real story about

Harmony – but then, *why would she? You were the one that said you'd come back, and you're the one that got caught kissing her.*

Heaving a sigh of resignation, he knew it was too late for him. She would never give him a second chance now.

Dallas watched from the doorway as Connor brushed his hair back from his forehead, wishing it was her hands sliding through the thick locks. She tugged at the hem of the black leather mini shirt trying for a modicum of decency, and then pulled the zipper on the black leather jacket down another inch.

Boy, she hoped this worked. Taking a deep breath, she braced herself for what was to come and quietly approached Connor. When she was directly behind him, she placed her hand lightly on his shoulder and whispered seductively, "Hi handsome, nice bike."

Connor froze, momentarily startled out of his self-berating. Not trusting that his mind wasn't playing tricks on him, he didn't turn around. He just slowly raised his head. In the mirror finish of the Harley's gas tank, he had a slightly distorted image of what looked like creamy colored breasts wrapped in black leather. The scent of exotic perfume wafted over him and through him.

He closed his eyes. Was he losing his grip on reality? Had he finally flipped out and begun hallucinating?

Opening them again, he looked. The vision was still there. Connor was afraid to turn around. He was afraid that this was a daydream; his desire for this to be real was overpowering.

"Connor...?"

Dallas was frightened. Connor hadn't moved. Hadn't acknowledged she was there. Did he hate her for not trusting him? For never returning his calls? For not giving him the chance to explain?

The seconds ticked off with agonizing slowness and still he didn't move. He didn't want her here. This blatant rebuff was his way of telling her.

Dallas slowly drew her hand away from his shoulder and straightened. The uncertainty of what to do next overwhelmed her.

What did I expect? That he would gather me into his arms and kiss me. Stupid woman, that's what you get for not trusting him – now leave before you make a bigger fool of yourself.

Dallas turned toward the door, but before she could take a step, a hand on her arm stopped her. "Dallas, don't go."

Tears shimmered, blurring her vision. "Why?"

She felt Connor tug on her wrist, forcing her to turn toward him. "Dallas, please look at me. Don't leave me again before I have a chance to explain."

Dallas tried to will her tears away and raised her eyes to Connor's, afraid of what she might see there. What she saw was her uncertainty mirrored in his eyes. Connor was just as afraid of *his* feelings as she was of hers.

Desire mixed with doubt, tempered with strong underlying emotions, caused her feelings to run close to the surface. She watched as he slowly ran his hand from her wrist to her upper arm, closing his fingers around her and drawing her closer.

"I'm sorry, Dallas. Sorry for everything that happened. For everything I said and didn't say. What you saw between me and Harmony was…"

Dallas put her fingertips to his lips. "It's okay, Connor.

Harmony told me everything. I've been such a fool. I should have let you explain. I should…"

The tears that Dallas had so valiantly held at bay slowly spilled down her cheeks. Her ability to speak was momentarily disabled. Love for the man that stood before her filled her heart.

In all the scenarios she had played in her mind, this was not the one that she had expected.

"Shhh, don't cry." Connor gently brushed the tears away with his thumbs. His hands cupped her face.

"I don't know what possessed Harmony to come to you and explain, but I'm damn glad she did. I know I did a lot of things wrong. I should have called you sooner. I should have told you how I felt." He paused.

"I know it's too late, but at least I'm glad you gave me this chance to apologize."

Dallas felt her whole world tilt on its axis. This sounded distinctly like a soul-cleansing good-bye. Not trusting herself to speak, Dallas' heart shattered again. Feeling foolish in her wild get-up and wearing her heart on her sleeve, all she wanted to do at this moment was get away.

Connor saw her withdraw from him emotionally and wondered why. He replayed his words, and he realized that what he had said could be mistaken for "goodbye".

Shit, how much more can I mess this up?

He cupped her face in his hands. "Dallas, I'm sorry. I'm not saying this right."

She tried to turn away, but Connor stepped closer.

"What I want to say is that I love you, and if you can

forgive me, I want to spend the rest of our lives showing you how much."

Did she hear right? Had he said he loved her?

Connor saw her hesitation, so he drew on the line of communication that had always worked for them. Grabbing her by the arms, he drew her up against his length.

"I love you, Dallas. I think I've loved you from the first moment I saw you."

Lowering his head, he captured her lips in a bone-melting, all-consuming kiss that left no doubt in her mind how much he loved her.

"I love you too, Connor. I love you too!"

The resounding cheer that went up from J.T. and the employees of Rev It Up filtered through to Connor and Dallas. Connor had a fleeting thought about killing J.T. for eavesdropping on this most personal moment, but it would have to wait.

Right now, all he wanted was to find out exactly what Dallas had on under her leather jacket.

EPILOGUE

THE WEDDING GUESTS all waved and cheered as Dallas and Connor left for their honeymoon. There were some who wondered why they wanted to spend it racing motorcycles for six days, but for those who knew the reason, it was more than appropriate.

Harmony Wells held the bride's bouquet gently in her arms. She was aware of the meaning behind the tradition, and she hoped it was true. The "Heirloom Bandit" case had brought her more than the gratification of a job well done. It had brought her Patrick.

Patrick Ryan smiled at the woman walking toward him. He had known from the moment he met her that she was special.

He took her hand, brought it to his lips, smiled, and said, "Ready to go?"

Harmony smiled back and gave a nod of her head. "Ready when you are."

She was taking a leave of absence from her job with the FBI so that she and Patrick could follow up on the piece of evidence that had been found. With any luck it would lead them to the missing Van Gogh.

Maybe, they would find more than the missing painting.

ACKNOWLEDGEMENTS

THIS BOOK HAS been a long time in the writing, and there are a few people that I would like to thank for encouraging me to take the step to publish it.

The first would be my late husband, who never discouraged me from trying new things. Thank you, my love.

I would also like to thank Joanne Welyki and her mother, Sally Chandler, the best beta-readers an author could ask for. They offered encouragement and gave me the strength to take the step to publish. I will always be grateful.

Thank you to my sons, Greg and Ryan, who understood why Mom was always locked in her office for hours.

And last, a thank you to Jackie Krstic, who was there at the beginning of this journey, giving ideas and insight.

The book has had many re-writes, but I believe that it is the best "ride" that Dallas could ask for.

CPSIA information can be obtained
at www.ICGtesting.com
Printed in the USA
BVHW080820020720
582412BV00002B/9

9 781525 562549